THE
EVOLUTION
OF MAN

SKYE WARREN

PROLOGUE

PLUS INTEREST

Dear Christopher,

Enclosed you'll find a formal offer to purchase the land and building of Bardot and Mayfair Development Parcel A, formerly known as the Tanglewood Library. Enclosed you will find terms equal to the last sale price plus interest. I hope you find this more than reasonable for a property that's currently sitting unused and half turned to rubble.

PS. And you know a library will help the community and revitalize the west side of the city.

Dear Harper,

I regret to inform you that the asking price of the property has increased significantly, due to recent media interest. A famous artist sparked a citywide protest that had its own hashtag. In fact looters were able to sell pieces of painted concrete for up to five thousand dollars online. As such Bardot and Mayfair cannot accept less than two billion dollars.

PS. I wonder how much concrete you'd have to sell to fill the library with new books?

Dear Christopher,

Twenty times what you paid for it? I hardly think the presence of some random painter with an Instagram account can possibly raise the value that much. Besides the fact that anyone will have to pay to reconstruct the entire front of the building, due to your wrecking ball.

PS. You are the most self-centered, arrogant bastard I've ever met.

Dear Harper,

Enclosed you'll find copies of the purchase offers this company has received in the months since we stopped development on the property. As you can plainly see, the presence and painting of a world-renowned, extremely talented artist has made the property invaluable.

PS. Don't sell yourself short.

CHAPTER ONE

REAL ESTATE

"WHAT DO YOU think?" the real estate agent asks, smiling bright-white teeth with a smudge of red lipstick. I can't blame her for being a little faded. We've been all over Tanglewood looking for the perfect house. There are Victorians and chateaus and three-story high-rise condominiums. There was a beautiful mid-century modern that I probably would have chosen.

This decision isn't up to me, though. Mom's the one who chooses.

She's the one who has to live here. And she's the one who has to die here.

I wander up the steps toward the white columns that line the front. "It's definitely big."

That's an understatement. Most of the houses in our price range are mansions, because we need the privacy more than the space. Large houses mean large grounds.

"Twelve bedrooms," the real estate agent assures me.

Mom leans to smell a wide, blooming hydrangea. "What are you going to do with all that space?"

"They'll be useful when we throw wild sex parties," I say lightly, because it's easier to pretend everything's fine than falling apart. "When people want privacy, they can go upstairs and leave a sock on the doorknob."

The real estate agent can't seem to figure out whether we're joking. She fumbles with the lock for a moment, trying to juggle her phone and a folder with notes about the house. "Five acres," she tells us. "And you saw the gate when we entered. The security system is completely updated."

She finally gets the door open, and we step inside.

Mom sucks in a breath. "Oh my God."

A large staircase covered in an antique rug curves up to a wide balcony. A chandelier made of crystal drops shimmers from the sunlight we're letting in. Elaborate wood paneling covers the wall, made especially intricate around an archway.

The real estate agent nods. "It's like the plantation house from *Gone with the Wind*. You can almost imagine that Scarlett will come running down the stairs with her sisters."

The movie was actually filmed near where we lived, in the backyard of the filming studios, the house left to rot away once it had served its purpose. In contrast this house seems vibrant. It's fitting that we would come from somewhere pretend to the real thing.

"Could you give us a minute?" I ask the agent.

When we're alone, my mother lets out a blissful sigh. "It's perfect."

"Will you be comfortable here?" I ask because that's all there is right now. Not time. Sand whips through the funnel at an alarming rate. There's only comfort, and how much my trust fund can buy.

She gives me a rueful smile. "Now that I've seen this, I can't imagine being comfortable anywhere else."

I look at the staircase dubiously. It's beautiful but not really practical, especially for someone who has stage four cancer. "Maybe we can have an elevator put in. Or one of those chairs that zooms along the balcony."

A horrified look. "Don't even think about it.

You will not do anything to destroy these stairs. It would be a travesty. They're so beautiful, Harper."

"Oh fine, I'm sure we can rig some kind of pulley system."

She laughs a little. "There won't be enough time to worry about it."

How can she laugh about this? It's one thing to be flippant in front of the real estate agent, but when we're like this, being honest, all I want to do is break down. My stomach flips over, and I have to look away through the arched doorway. "God."

"I'm sorry," she says, immediately contrite. "I know this is hard for you."

"No," I tell her, because hard is a test on calculus. Hard is knowing I'll inevitably see Sutton or Christopher again. This is more than hard; it's unbearable. "I'm the one who's sorry. We can buy this house, stairs or elevator or pulley system. Or hell, we can buy the original set back in LA, if that's what you want. We'll still be able to get fresh wheatgrass delivered every morning."

She smiles. "We should be here."

My throat tightens up, because no matter how hard I try, I seem to mess this up. She could have asked me for every cent in the damn trust fund. I'd have climbed the highest mountain or crawled into the deepest cave to find a cure. Instead she asked for something else—acceptance.

"Why Tanglewood? You never even visited here before this week."

"Because this city has what you need."

I scrunch my nose. "The library? I don't need to oversee the reconstruction personally."

"Nonsense. This is your project. You should be here for it. And besides, it's not only the library. Tanglewood has the people you love."

"Mom, I told you—"

"You do love Avery, don't you?" she asks, sounding completely innocent. "She's your best friend, and she's taking the semester off to work on her thesis. That means she'll be in town."

My throat feels tight. "I'm not going to suddenly get married and have a baby."

My mom has never pushed me to settle down, because she knows the dangers of that more than anyone. And now she'll never see me walk down the aisle. Never meet any grandchildren. The doctors have given her three to six months to live. Three to six months. How do they even calculate that?

There might have been three more months if she'd been willing to try their grueling treatment—or ironically, the treatment could have killed her faster.

She's asked me to accept her decision, and mostly I have. There isn't a protest I can stage that will change her mind. I've accepted it, but that doesn't make it any less painful to bear.

"And Bea," she murmurs, still pretending to be clueless. We're staying with Bea and Hugo in their comfy penthouse until we find our own place. "You love her and Hugo. They're a darling couple."

I give her a droll look. "Is that the end of the list?"

"For now. I'm sure you'll learn to love more people once you've lived in Tanglewood longer."

The banister shakes a little when I touch it, and I think we'll have to get a carpenter in here before it's safe enough to move in. If my mother wants a grand staircase to descend every morning, then that's what she'll get. I can't give her relief from the pain, but my God, I can give her stairs.

"I messed it up," I whisper because she needs to understand.

I don't know how to love someone without the taint of money. I don't know how to have a relationship with a man where I'm not waiting for him to leave. There's something dangerous inside me; it grows and grows, eating away at everything good and hopeful and trusting. I don't know if I ever loved Sutton, if I ever could have loved him, but we didn't get that far.

And as for Christopher? I'm not sure he's capable of loving anyone.

Her hand covers mine on the gleaming banister. "Harper."

The softness of her voice reaches deep inside me. We've lived in a hundred different houses. None of them were ever ours. They belonged to one of her husbands. Some of those men were upfront about not wanting a little stepdaughter underfoot. Others pretended to be interested in me. They bought me Barbie doll limos and stuffed dogs with puppies inside them, but eventually they were all the same.

They all kicked us out in the end.

"You don't have to make my mistakes," she says, except her eyes are the same hazel gold as my own. It's like looking in a mirror. She's somehow more beautiful with age, but it doesn't make her happy.

"Don't I?" I didn't get left behind by one man, but two. She only knows about Sutton, but when I close my eyes there's two men walking away from me. I have enough distance from what happened six months ago to know it was

Christopher who I really wanted. Enough distance to know that Sutton is the closest I've ever come to really having love, the kind that is given and received and untarnished by money. I had him, and I let him go.

"Love isn't supposed to be painful."

"Then why does it hurt?" Christopher never did anything so mundane, so hopeful as ask me on a date. He never offered himself to me, so why did I keep choosing him?

Her small smile tears my heart in two. "I'm hoping you figure that out the way that I never could. I fell in love with the wrong man, hard enough that there was never any real chance with me and someone else after that. There's still time for you, Harper."

"I'm not here to date anyone. And definitely not Sutton."

She makes a noncommittal sound. "Everything will work out."

Except my mother has stage four cancer and refuses treatment. The library is broken beyond repair. Everything in my life is falling apart, so how will it work out? I touch a carved wood finial that's part of the railing. It's easier to lie when I'm not looking at her. "Okay."

"Harper. Look at me."

It takes me five seconds. I count down in my head. I can't take anything for granted these days—not the ability to stand up straight or hold my head high. Not the ability to look at my mother without incriminating tears burning my eyes.

She gives me a gentle smile. "I talked to a hospice in the city."

My heart does a strange pitter-patter, like it's beating enough times for a year but all at once and uneven. Heat and cold courses through me, one after the other. It's like my body's electrical system is shorting out. "I thought you didn't want that."

"I don't want to live there, but they have a home-based program."

"What does that mean?"

"Well, they have nurses who come help me."

"I can do that." Even though helping means watching my mom lose her functionality, piece by piece. Two weeks ago I had to help her open a jar of unsweetened organic peanut butter. And then I hid in the pantry and cried for two hours.

"You're not here to wait on me," she says with a laugh. "Anyway, I spoke to the care transition counselor on the phone. She's coming to the house later this week so we can work on the

Death Plan. That's what they call it. Isn't that funny?"

All the crazy electrical voltage disappears. There's a flat line where my heartbeat had been. I might as well be made of stone, that's how numb I feel suddenly. "What?"

"It's just a name, Harper."

"I'm not—No—"

"This is something that will help all of us. Especially you."

"I will buy this house and I will live here and I will do anything you want, but I'm not going to make a Death Plan." Even the library is a kind of tribute, whether she knows it or not—fixing the unfixable, bringing it back from the brink. I had to accept my mother's decision to stop treatment, but that doesn't mean I'm going to embrace her death. I'm not going to *plan* for it.

CHAPTER TWO

DEEP POCKETS

THERE ARE VERY few things in my control right now. I make only a single demand in the purchase of the library—that Christopher Bardot meet with me personally. I want him to look me in the eye when he signs these documents. Part of me is afraid of what I'll find, but I need to know. Did he ever care about me? He manipulated me to save the library, only to hold it hostage for a hefty chunk of my trust fund. The same trust fund he fought so hard to protect. He's an enigma wrapped in a mystery, and I'm determined to peel away at least a few layers at our meeting.

His acceptance comes back in the form of a hand-couriered, notarized letter. He agrees to the meeting, it says, as long as it happens at a restaurant of his choosing.

saw me last week instead of six months ago.

"Christopher," I say, in case he hasn't noticed. A table like this is reserved for VIPs or very special guests. Or ones with deep pockets. "This is the chef's table. We're sitting at the chef's table in Koi."

"Is that good? I thought they just ran out of regular tables."

"Did you just make a joke. Oh my God. You did."

The chef chooses that moment to introduce himself, a rather effusive man with a comforting smile and a thick Japanese accent. He says he'll forgive that we drink champagne as long as we try the sake pairing he sends with every course. And he personally serves the amuse bouche, a tuna sashimi lollie on a fennel cilantro salad with ponzu dressing that makes me moan despite myself.

"Dear God," I say when we're alone again, my eyes still closed with the wonder of that single bite. There's salt and citrus, and basically this is what heaven tastes like. "Did you spend all two billion dollars to get this table? Because it's worth it."

When I open my eyes Christopher is watching me, a strange expression on his face. He hasn't touched the plate in front of him. He seems more interested in the way that I dip my finger in the ponzu dressing and lime foam to savor the last drops. I'm not sure that love is on the table, but if the glitter in his eyes is anything to go by, sex is definitely an option.

"One billion," he says, almost absently.

I blink. "What?"

"Only one billion is mine. The other half belongs to Sutton."

It's like a bucket of cold water dumped over my head. "Why did you bring me here?"

One dark eyebrow rises. "You're the one who insisted we meet in person."

"And you're the one who brought me here."

The long pause that follows isn't filled with hearts and roses. He does not secretly love me, and I feel like a fool for even considering the possibility. Because he took me out to dinner? It's really a good thing I don't date much, because I'm terrible at it.

"I invested in the restaurant," he says finally. "It helps to have your take."

"Because I have such a refined palate?"

"Because you were born rich," he says, his voice flat. "You know what rich people like."

It takes my breath away, and I'm left staring at

him with the most incredible taste on my tongue. That's all I am to him? A rich girl with nothing better to do with my time than give him advice on his new restaurant? Meanwhile I was gullible enough to think he actually wanted to spend time with me. It isn't right. It isn't fair, but then Christopher Bardot has never played fair.

The chef returns with an oyster for each of us, with a strawberry fish sauce, compressed strawberries, and coriander blossoms. It's definitely the most beautiful oyster I've ever seen. Christopher is the one who takes a bite first, letting it slide into his mouth in a graceful movement. He closes his eyes, clearly enjoying the taste, and my cheeks turn warm as I realize I must have looked like this when I ate the amuse bouche—like someone having an orgasm.

I have actually had sex with Christopher Bardot but sitting to the side in the busy kitchen of a hip restaurant, watching him make that face feels like watching something private.

And regardless of whether he wants my rich-person opinion of the restaurant, I have no desire to sit here and be turned on by a man who doesn't even like me.

"The papers," I manage to say, my voice a little hoarse. I have to clear my throat and try it again, before they come out clear enough to understand. "Where are the papers?"

"Try the oyster," he says, and because I'm weak, I'm so weak, I actually do.

I have a feeling this evening is going to crash and burn and I *really* want to taste the oyster. It slides onto my tongue with a burst of flavor, the strawberries almost unrecognizable this way, tart and lush and cold. It's like a crisp bite of the ocean. *Oh God.* My eyes close. I'm making the face. I *know* I'm making the face, but I can't stop. It's so good.

When I actually open my eyes again, my muscles are lax. My defenses are down. It's like I really did have an orgasm right here in this black wooden chair with mother-of-pearl inlays along the sides. Pleasure still lingers in my body, like warm honey on the inside.

"I didn't bring them," Christopher says, and it's like another ice-water bucket.

"Are you serious? Why not?"

"I forgot."

"I don't think you've forgotten anything the entire time I've known you. You probably have a photographic memory, don't you? There's no way you forgot."

A shrug. "Maybe."

"Is this a game to you?" I left my mother in the *Gone with the Wind* house by herself, and I know she'll be fine without me for a few hours. But something could happen. Inevitably something *will* happen, and this man is playing around with my time like it's nothing.

"A game." He seems to consider it seriously. "No. It's not fun enough for a game."

I stand up, throwing my napkin down on the empty oyster shell. "You know what? Go ahead and mail me the papers. I don't know why I asked to meet with you. You are worse than self-centered, Christopher. Worse than arrogant. Now you're just downright mean."

CHAPTER THREE

PILE OF RUBBLE

I T NEVER CEASES to surprise me that I tumble headfirst into holes that I've dug myself.

Or in this case, tripped over a piece of concrete that I painted in peaceful protest, which caused a halt to the construction of a shiny new strip mall where an abandoned library had stood. The marble floor catches my fall, sending shocks of pain up my arms and knees.

"Are you okay?" Avery asks, peering from the heavy plastic tarp behind me.

"Never better," I say, dusting my hands off. "But watch your step."

She glances around the large space with those wide Bambi eyes. God, no wonder Gabriel Miller went after this woman. He would have wanted her even if she hadn't auctioned off her virginity like fresh meat in the middle of the forest. "Are you sure it's safe to be here?"

It's definitely not safe. "I'm sure no one's going to stop us. They mostly put up the barricades because people kept stealing pieces of concrete, which is crazy considering there are shelves full of old and rare books inside."

"The concrete was selling for so much money online," Avery says, her tone overly reasonable. "Then there was that one chunk with Cleopatra's eye—"

"Can we not talk about that?"

"The bidding got to five figures, didn't it?"

I glare at her. "We're here to talk about construction plans, right?"

She bends to examine a small piece of concrete where an inch of white paint remains. "You have to own the building before you can start construction."

"Oh, I own it."

"Christopher sold it to you?" She sounds surprised.

It surprised me, too. Christopher Bardot might be cold and arrogant, but he has a strict moral code. Strict enough that he would never steal from my trust fund. That's what I thought, until he made a veritable fortune selling me a pile of concrete. It makes me feel betrayed, which in turn makes me feel foolish, because I know better than to trust a man.

"All for the low bargain price of two billion dollars."

Her mouth drops open. "What?"

My smile feels grim. "That's what it's worth now. I had independent appraisers confirm it. It's definitely the most expensive pile of rubble I've ever seen."

We cross the room together in silence—hers thoughtful, mine full of useless frustration. Losing the money doesn't bother me. The fact that Christopher demanded it does.

The heavy plastic sheeting blocks out most of the light from the front, leaving only the broken stained-glass atrium shining down on us. There are still sheets of paper in stacks on the circular desk. Still a few books stacked haphazardly. Still the wall—carved with industrious people mingling with the four elements.

"It's beautiful," Avery breathes.

Her taste runs more to Hellenic art, but I knew she'd appreciate the wall. Beautiful, even though it has a huge crack in the middle. It looks like a wound in flesh, a gash made from some giant from one of her Greek myths wielding an ancient weapon.

Twenty feet of butternut wood carvings climb the back of the library. It feels like a single, impossibly large slab of wood even though it's constructed like puzzle pieces—stylized waves jutting against wheat-filled plains, an angled man wielding an ax set against a bursting sunrise. It fits together as if drawn in smooth strokes, made from imagination and sheer will instead of months of painstaking labor.

I touch the tip of a wood-made ocean wave, almost a caress. "This piece belongs to the community. The way they work and break and hope. You can feel its heart here."

"I can feel it beating," she says, awed.

"It was about two minutes and twenty feet from being a pile of splinters."

She traces a constellation with her forefinger. "God. Lucky you were here, then. I don't think anyone could have saved it except you. You are the only one crazy enough to do it."

Her voice has reverence, taking the sting out of the observation. And I understand where she's coming from. I'm the one who buys a multi-million dollar antebellum mansion because my mother likes the columns in the front. I'm the one who stages a protest on the steps of an old library. That's Harper, someone you can count on to be over the top.

I glance toward the front of the library, where most of the wall and glass doors have crumbled. The wrecking ball didn't reach all the way to the back wall, but it still managed to harm it. It was sold as a teardown property, only useful for the land to rebuild something new.

My over-the-top ideas aren't always practical.

"So far I haven't found a construction company willing to take on the project. They're insisting the only thing to do is bulldoze it."

The building itself seems to shudder, on the verge of collapse. It wasn't like this when I left it six months ago, but it wouldn't have mattered. The purchase price is based on razing the library to the ground, on turning the carvings into sawdust. This is my chance to save it.

The men in these carvings build and lift and break. They don't bow to the land, but they're yoked to it all the same, strong and somehow surrendered. These men in their newsboy caps and heavy boots shouldn't be familiar, but they are. The potent drive inside them that makes them human, the limitless thirst for something more.

"I can't stop looking at it," she says, her gaze lifted.

God, they shouldn't remind me of modern-day men with their suits and their cunning. Their limitless ambition for things they weren't born with. They shouldn't soften me toward Christopher Bardot, because that would make me vulnerable. Again.

I touch the wide gouge, a sympathetic throb of pain in my finger. "It's a survivor."

She nods as if I've said something profound. "You're right, but it's more than that. Survival is about staying the same. This piece is about yearning."

My stomach clenches, because it's useless to yearn. Didn't I learn that after watching Daddy marry over and over while my mother struggled to pay the rent?

Didn't I learn that after wanting two men and ending up alone?

She's right though. The way the men rise above their struggles, the way they reach even higher. It's a monument to longing, which is terrifying, because that can only lead to disappointment.

I snatch my hand back, determined to hide the strange tightening in my chest.

Walking through a high archway, I step deeper into the library. All the construction people I talked to seemed to agree: the part of the building with the books is the most stable. Unfortunately they also agree that the main hall, the part with the gorgeous stained-glass dome at the top, the priceless carved wall, the rare blue-gold marble mosaic floor, is not.

Avery gasps when she follows me. It's an impressive sight, all this history. All these stories. How many hands turned the pages? How many questions were answered?

She runs her fingers across the spines. "Fairy tales," she moans, sounding almost orgasmic. "There's a whole section for fairy tales. I could die right here."

"Please don't. Gabriel would definitely kill me."

Dust rises in the air as she pulls a faded cloth-bound book from the shelf. "Once upon a time, there was a miller who had a beautiful daughter," she reads, her forefinger on the yellowed page. "He told the king his daughter could spin straw into gold."

"What I never understood about this story is, why would he lie? It seems like something that would be easy enough to verify. Didn't he know that would come next?"

She shrugs. "It's not really about the miller.

The story is about his daughter."

"The one who can't spin straw into gold."

A sudden grin. "That's kind of what you did, isn't it? Turned those pieces of concrete and splashes of paint into gold. That's pretty magical of you, miller's daughter."

I groan. "You aren't going to let that go, are you?"

"Nope."

"The only reason my protest was such big news is because Christopher tried to tear down the library. He's the one who gave me the cause to protest."

"Like Rumpelstiltskin," she says, her tone musing. "She could only do it with his help."

A horrible thought occurs to me. A horrible, terrible, painful thought. One that makes my limbs turn cold. "Oh my God, did he do it on purpose? Was that his plan all along?"

"What are you talking about?"

"He knew I would stage the protest and then the land would be worth more, which would give him way more profit and a lot faster than actually developing it." Christopher made more money this way than his stupid mall—and he made it a lot faster, too.

She looks dubious. "That would be really…

diabolical."

"Exactly. He's *so* diabolical. If we look up the word 'diabolical' in one of the old dictionaries here, there will be Christopher's face with his dark eyes and cheekbones."

"His cheekbones." She snorts. "I don't know if he did it on purpose, but if he did... well, it's interesting that he knows you that well. Well enough to predict what you'd do."

Interesting? No, it's terrible. Because I don't know that man at all. I never thought he'd use me. I believed him when he said he wanted to build that shiny new mall. Believed him when he said he planned to tear down the library.

And I believed him when he said he wouldn't hurt me.

"Do you really think he did it on purpose?" Avery asks softly, her soft gaze on the old ink. "It would have been easier to just siphon money out of your trust fund."

I wrap my arms around myself. Is it possible? Avery's gaze is warm and concerned. The certainty settles deep inside me, a knot in my stomach. Yes, it's very possible. Likely, even.

He used me. He predicted what I would do.

"Christopher isn't the kind of man who wants things easy. He would have considered that cheating. But manipulating people? He considers that fair game. He knows I've protested before. Only this time I had connections and a social media platform. And voila!"

"He isn't your father," Avery says softly.

"Isn't he?" Another man who values money over kindness, who places his ambition ahead of the women in his life. "He could have sold me the library for what they paid for it. He could have doubled the sale price and still made a nice profit."

The realization puts a stop to whatever fantasy I'd been spinning in my head about Christopher Bardot suddenly realizing he were in love with me. I kind of wish we were at Koi again, just so I could throw another oyster shell in his face.

After I've swallowed what's inside of course. It was too delicious to waste.

Her nose scrunches. "It is kind of mean."

A shiver runs through me, because that's what I called him last night. Mean. Has he crossed the same Rubicon that my father did? Or was Christopher always this way, with me too wide-eyed infatuated to know it? "How are you and Gabriel?" I ask because I need to hear something positive. There's a rich and ambitious man who doesn't think loving someone makes him weak.

Those two are crazy in love, despite their wicked beginning—or maybe because of it.

"We're good." She closes the book of fairy tales and walks back into the main hall.

Surprise freezes me where I stand. It takes me a full minute to follow her and demand an explanation. "Good. Good? What happened to *I love Gabriel, he's the best, and he gives me so many orgasms?*"

A blush darkens her cheeks. "Well, there are still orgasms."

"Does he snore?" I ask sympathetically.

"What? No."

"Don't tell me he forgot your anniversary."

"It's not that." A notch forms between her eyebrows. "At least I don't think so. I'm pretty bad with dates actually. It's just that he's been working so much lately. And traveling a lot."

Unease moves through my stomach. "I thought he came with you to Tanglewood."

She's a graduate student at Smith College, working toward her doctorate, only here at the tail end of summer break. He's a businessman with international investments. There are natural struggles to them being together, but they always seemed ridiculously happy. Always kissing and snuggling—and Gabriel is not the natural snuggling type.

He can't seem to help himself with Avery. Or at least he couldn't before.

"I'm sure it will be fine," she says in a too-bright voice. "Besides, if he were here, he never would have let me come to the library. This place looks like it's about to fall down on our heads."

A bird flies in through the atrium above us, disturbing a few shards of the stained-glass window that used to protect us. They fall down with a long dive to the ground, landing in a pile of other rubble. Dust follows it down in a light flurry of exclamation. No, the building hasn't gone unscathed from the wrecking ball. There are cracks in the very heart of it.

CHAPTER FOUR

GOLD RUSH

I N FIFTH GRADE my friend had a birthday party at her family's country house, where the stables were climate-controlled and the horses had elaborate braids in their manes. That place bears no resemblance to the massive stable behind the house, its doors wide open to welcome the sun, the packed ground somehow more comfortable than a glossy synthetic flooring. Horses stand in clean bays, watching me with lazy curiosity from their sideways eyes.

Another set of wide-open doors leads me back outside.

Paddocks link across the land as far as the eye can see, connected by high rustic wood gates and bristling with a kind of raw potential. This is a place where nature still holds her power, where man tests himself against her and sometimes loses.

A glint of light off metal. My gaze snaps to a large paddock at the base of a hill. I'm drawn toward it as if pulled by an invisible string, the thread made of reluctant excitement and a base female instinct to seek strength.

There's a horse in the middle of the paddock, its body held taut, the stomp of its foreleg nervous. A pale blonde and white dappled coat makes her look otherworldly. I don't have experience with horses beyond birthday parties and Renaissance fair pony rides, but there's no doubt in my mind that this is still a wild animal— which means the man who wants to tame her is in danger. A free spirit doesn't want to be broken.

Sutton strolls in a wide arc, his posture deceptively relaxed, his blue eyes alert on the animal penned in with him. His heather-gray T-shirt clings to his muscles, the back darker with sweat. Worn jeans sketch the powerful lines of his thighs better than a bespoke suit ever could.

"Whoa there," he's saying, his voice low and soothing. "I'm not going to hurt you, beautiful. You're safe here. We'll take as long as you need to believe it."

God, no wonder this man can tame horses. I'm halfway pliant from hearing him murmur promises of safety and patience. There's something unique about Sutton, a core of absolute sincerity, a sensation deep in my bones that I can trust him.

"Do the horses ever talk back?" I say, my voice soft. I'm careful not to make any sudden movements as I loop my arm over the thick plank of wood.

Sutton doesn't seem the least surprised to hear me, which confirms my suspicion that he knew I was here. Even though he doesn't take his eyes from the horse, his attention encompasses the whole of the paddock. The whole of the land. It encompasses me.

The corner of his mouth lifts. "Who says I was talking to the horse?"

That surprises a laugh out of me. Always this man can surprise me, beguile me. Tease me into wanting something I've told myself would never work. "How long have you had her?"

"A few months," he says, taking another few steps to the side, coming an inch away from touching her before moving away. "But I've only just started taking her out. She had abrasions on her legs when I got her, and a lung infection that hadn't been treated."

Unease moves through my stomach as I look at the beautiful animal. She's dangerous and strong... and healthy. It hurts to imagine her as anything else. And underneath the rebelliousness I sense the dark tinge of fear.

"Someone hurt her?"

"They neglected her," he says, his voice flat. "Which is the same thing when she needs to be taken care of. A friend of mine found her in a stall with someone he was doing business with. Bought her because he couldn't stand to see the conditions she was living in. Almost put her down before he thought to call me."

Steel squeezes my heart. "Put her down?"

Sutton takes another few steps, passing close enough to touch her but choosing not to. The horse snorts her protest but doesn't move away from him. It strikes me that this is a dance, the athleticism and grace unmistakable, purpose imbued into his every movement.

"It takes quite a bit of money to take care of a horse. Especially one who already has health problems. One who will still need to be broken."

His matter-of-fact tone takes my breath away. Does he think about people that way, too? Does he think about *me* that way? "Is that how you see her?"

"Of course not. That's why—"

The pounding of my heart fills my ears.

"With a dollar sign over her head? And if her medicine costs more than that, what's the point of keeping her alive? She's disposable anyway."

Sutton walks toward me, and suddenly I'm backing away. The safety I had felt on the other side of the fence evaporates beneath his piercing blue eyes. He ducks between the horizontal slats, coming toward me, making me back away until I finally remember to stand my ground. Then we're face-to-face, and I'm confronted with the sheer size of him. In the paddock it had been theoretical, more like artwork to be admired. Standing in front of me, he breathes and moves with potent hunger. More than something to be wanted, he's someone who *wants.*

"That's not how I see her," he says, his tone gentle.

"I'm sorry," I say, breathless. "Of course you don't. You're taking care of her."

"She has a home here. Even if she never lets me ride."

"Okay," I say, my chest tight.

His eyes pierce my armor, seeing the secret fear I've worked hard to protect. That I'm only a series of numbers preceded by a dollar sign. That I'm a living, breathing line-item entry in a spreadsheet, no matter how much I pretend to be worth more than that.

"I'm surprised you're even speaking to me," he says, his gaze turning dark. He looks at my lips for a moment. "Figured you'd be pissed about the price tag for the library."

"I thought you weren't part of the company anymore."

"Resigned my position, which means I didn't have a say. But I still owned my share of the company and profited from the deal that Bardot made with you."

"It was his decision to be an asshole. I just wish I hadn't played into his hand."

"Then why are you still doing it?" The words are soft, but they fall like bullets.

"I'm not."

"You think he doesn't want you back in Tanglewood? Back in the library?"

"He doesn't care what I do." I'm doing this for my mother, because I will do almost anything for her. Except for meet with the person from the hospice to help make her Death Plan. The name makes me shiver. *Hurt and hurt and hurt, and then die.* We don't need a plan.

We need a time machine.

A quiet laugh. "Christopher Bardot is far from indifferent. He's developing the luxury condominiums right next to the library, and guess who lives on the top floor?"

I stare at him, disbelieving. But even while my mind refuses to accept this, my body turns warm. "Whatever happens next to the library isn't my problem. I'm only concerned with restoring it. Will you help me? It's important for the city."

And no one else will take the job.

Every construction company I've tried has told me to tear down the building and start again. The words *not structurally sound* have been used more than once. If I were smart, I would actually listen to them, but I'm the queen of lost causes.

Sutton looks away, toward the land. "I can't say no to you, but it isn't for the good of the damned city. And it's not even for Christopher Bardot. Not anymore."

"Why would you have done it for Christopher?"

He smiles without humor. "Why indeed?"

I take a step toward him, close enough that I have to look up to meet the sky blue of his eyes. "You never did tell me why you went into business with him."

"My reasons don't matter."

That's the only warning before his head lowers, before his lips touch mine. Warm. Insistent.

He kisses me the way the sun shines on the land, certain of its welcome. My body opens toward him in instinctive surrender, pleasure washing over me in waves.

As quickly as he claimed me, he's gone again. He steps back, leaving a cool breeze between us. There's nothing sensual or intimate in his expression.

I touch my lips as if I can hold some of his warmth there. I told myself I wasn't interested in dating, but I can't deny that I want this intimacy. It feels like breathing after being so long underwater. It feels like air. His blue eyes track the movement, hungry, belying the air of indifference in his stance.

"You stopped," I say, a little relieved, mostly sad. "Because I kissed Christopher?"

"That was a wake-up call for me, but no. I'm not angry with you, if that's what you're asking. You can kiss whoever you want. And I'm the last person to judge you."

"Then why—"

"I'll restore the library because you asked me to. Like I said, my reasons don't really matter. But I can't be with you, Harper. Not like before. I can't go there again."

My stomach lurches. I would have said I already knew that. That I'm not looking to be with any man, but the rejection hurts all the same. "Before, when you courted me."

A slight nod.

That was the word he used. Courted. It only stopped when he found Christopher kissing me. And me kissing him back. Sutton may claim not to be angry about it, but what other reason could there be for him pulling back? Why else would he have left?

"That's good," I manage to say. And I almost mean it.

I've always been the girl every boy chased. The one who could always walk away.

I *needed* to be that girl so that I could keep myself safe, so that I would never end up desperate and alone and scared like my mother. Then two men made me fall for them. Hard. They both walked away at the same time. And look, I could handle the hit to my pride. I can pull up my big girl panties to deal with the humiliation of that.

It's the blows they dealt to my heart that left me broken. Shattered. I'm like a cartoon statue that's been hammered. There's a crack at the impact. The crack spreads into a thousand fractures, until I'm made of a million pieces.

There's a moment in the show when I'm frozen in air that way, and that's how I've been living these past six months—the pieces suspended, waiting to fall. There's no way to avoid it; the killing blow already happened.

For a moment he looks bereft. "Good," he repeats.

It breaks my heart a little, that this handsome, virile, charming man would doubt himself. That I ever let him think I wanted Christopher instead of him. "You were enough for me, Sutton. You were enough for anyone."

He gives a slight shake of his head as if waking from a dream. "It doesn't matter. There's nothing between us except the library now. Nothing holding us together anymore."

It makes me wonder what had held us together before. Attraction? Chemistry? We'd had those in spades, but I remember the wry tone when he'd said, *I'm the last person to judge you.* It makes me wonder if it had been Christopher binding us together all along.

"There's something I should tell you. The library…" My breath catches. "It's more than a restoration. More than rebuilding the front wall. It's in bad shape. I think the wrecking ball made the building weaker, in places we can't even see."

He studies me. "Are you saying you think I can't save it?"

We aren't only talking about the library. "I'm asking you to try."

"And if it can't be saved?"

The thought sucks the air out of my body, leaving me hollow and thin. There are only two things I've fought for—my mother's life and the library. It's only a matter of time before I lose the first one. I can't bear to lose the other one, too. It would break me.

Some of my despair must show on my face, because Sutton's jaw clenches. "How bad are we talking, Harper?"

"You aren't my first stop. I asked every construction company in Tanglewood to look at the library. None of them would even bid on it. They said it has to be destroyed."

I'M EXPECTING A construction crew complete with cranes and drills and whatever else they use to fix old libraries. Instead it's just Sutton driving a black Explorer, pulling up in the small parking lot between the library and the wasteland that is the west side of the city.

He tells me he has to take a look at the building before he can call a crew and give them information, so I wander through the shelves while he pokes around in the back rooms and climbs into the attic. He comes out smelling of dust and mothballs.

"So what do you think?" I know I must look too hopeful. I sound too hopeful, like someone who doesn't see that the building is literally falling down around us. It might be asking for a miracle, but when you're staring death in the face, that's what you need.

He looks up at the broken stained-glass window. "Harper."

"I mean I know it's kind of a mess." A strange little laugh escapes me. "It's actually missing the whole front wall. And there's all this rubble everywhere. I'm sure we can sweep that up."

Blue eyes darken. "Harper."

"And then there's the whole foundation issues. I'm not saying it will be easy."

"I need you to tell me why. Why do you want to do this?"

"Why *don't* I want to do this, that should be the question. Because it will be amazing for the community. Did you notice all the buildings falling down around us? The crime rate around here is… well, you know, it's bad. Books are the answer to that, Sutton."

A long pause and then with exasperation he says, "*Harper.*"

"Okay." I close my eyes tight. "Okay. I'll tell you. But I don't even fully understand it myself. I just know that there are only two things I care about—my mother and this library. I can't lose both of them." I already lost my father. I already lost Christopher and Sutton. People leave, but I can at least save the building. I can at least have smooth wood and concrete.

He looks away again, this time toward the wall. "Even if I agree to take on this project, even if I try to save the building, you understand there's a chance it won't work. Hell, we shouldn't even be standing here without support beams and hard hats. This whole thing could come crashing down on our heads."

I can't help my squeal of delight. "So you'll take the job!"

"I didn't say that."

That makes me hop around and clap. "You're totally going to do it. Thank you, thank you, thank you. You don't know how much this means to me."

He looks grim. "I think I actually might."

I stretch up on my toes and kiss his cheek. "I knew I could count on you. Everyone was like, no one would be crazy enough to take on this project." I use my best asshole-contractor voice. "And I was like, you know who'd be crazy enough?"

"Sutton Mayfair."

"That's right, Sutton Mayfair."

He turns serious. "How's your mother?"

My stomach knots the way it always does when I think of her. "They say she has six months to live. I don't understand how they calculate that. A hundred and eighty days."

"Are you sure you wouldn't rather spend the time with her? The library will be here when you're ready to work on it. You don't have to do this now."

There's a shudder, and then a rain of dusty concrete falls on us. Sutton pushes me under the circular library desk. The feel of his hands on something so innocuous as my arms, and suddenly I'm flashing back to the time he bent me over the desk. So much has changed since then. I thought I might be able to save my mother with impossible treatments.

I still had hope.

I'm not sure the library really would be here in six months, if we didn't do this now. The building is dying. My mother is dying. There's only one hundred and eighty days left.

"I'm not going to be the one drilling holes in the floors," I say softly. "That will be you and whoever you're working with. I only want to save the wall. If I can do that, if I can fix that terrible crack with my own two hands—"

I break off and stare at my hands, the nails cracked from the woodwork I've been testing out. My palms rough and calloused from years of painting. These are not delicate hands.

"I have to do something," I whisper, and it's like a confessional under that circular desk. "I have to fix something, and I think I might be the one running out of time."

CHAPTER FIVE

BLACKBALLED

THERE'S AN ENIGMA among painters. Let's say an artist studies and practices for twenty-five years of her life. Then she spends two hours painting a masterpiece. So did it take her two hours to create it? Or twenty-five years?

I don't know the answer to that, but I do know that sculpting a wall three stories high would take my entire life. There are splinters in my palm, open cuts on my fingers, and a deep purple bruise on my thumb caused by a rogue mallet. The block of oak looks more like a child's forgotten pile of Play-Doh than the angular bison I'm trying to re-create.

A pigeon flies across the open space, landing on an old green dust-covered lamp. The whole building seems to shift and sigh, as if its alive. As if it's hurting.

Sutton spent the past week with structural engineers and contractors who told him the same thing they told me—the library is broken beyond repair. While it stands now, the essence of the building is too weak to hold forever. And once construction begins, with its banging and its jostling, the whole thing might come down. It's a hazard. An accident waiting to happen.

Which is why I didn't tell Sutton that I was coming today.

He drove to his ranch today to work with Gold Rush. That's the name of the white-beige horse with fear and defiance in her eyes. If he's gone too long, he would lose her trust. That's what he told me last night when he called. He also told me that the library is a hopeless cause.

I study the grain of the wood, the way it fought the trowel.

There are woodworkers more qualified than me. Really any of them are more qualified than me. I've done basic sculpture as part of my degree and even used small wood pieces in some of my mixed media work. Nothing on this scale, but I can't give up the project. Even as much as I trust Sutton to save the building, as much as I hope he actually will, the wall has to be mine.

Maybe it's becoming an obsession.

As much of an obsession as the shiny mall had been to Christopher.

"What are you doing here?"

I turn back to see him stepping through the plastic sheeting, his eyes black with fury. It's like I've conjured him from my mind. He can't be real. Can't. Be. Even as he kicks aside pieces of debris and storms closer, even as the dust parts for him like the goddamn Red Sea, I'm sure he's part of my imagination. I must have inhaled more varnish than I thought.

He grasps my arms, both of them, hauling me up. I gasp at the sudden movement. The trowel I was holding clatters to the floor. Those black eyes sear me, accusatory and cold.

"I said, what the hell are you doing here?"

"Rumpelstiltskin," is all I can manage to say, which makes me sound crazy.

Christopher Bardot has always had that effect on me. From the time I was fifteen years old, he made me stutter and stumble. But he doesn't disappear when I say his name.

Instead he looks incredulous. "This building should be condemned."

I yank away from him, only able to breathe again when he's no longer touching me. "This building is none of your concern. Not after you sold it to me. For a ridiculous price, I should mention."

"It's my concern if it crashes to the ground next to *my* luxury condos."

"Oh no." I manage a laugh that sounds haughty and unafraid. As if I'm not shaking inside. "Sutton told me you're still developing in the west end. I'll stay out of your business if you stay out of mine."

His lips press together. It's as if the words are torn from him. As if each one pulls a piece of his skin when he speaks it. "When did you speak to Sutton?"

"When I hired him to restore the library."

"Restore. *Restore?* It's not a goddamn painting in a museum. It's a building that isn't structurally sound. There's no way you can get a contractor to work on it."

My eyes narrow. "Wait a second. Did you *talk* to contractors about this building?"

"Of course I talked to them," he says, his voice clipped. "I owned it."

"You bastard."

"The only thing to do is raze the building and start over."

"You *bastard*. You blackballed me. Told the contractors not to do business with me. What did you offer them? Some of the money I paid for the library? God. You are unbelievable."

"They're welcome to accept any job they find suitable."

"That's the only reason you sold it to me, isn't it? Because you knew I wouldn't be able to restore it." For two billion dollars. He sold me the library knowing I couldn't fix it.

"You can rebuild. Make it look exactly like it did before, if you want."

"It won't be the same."

"You're damn right it won't be the same. It will be structurally sound."

"Well, the joke is on you, because Sutton already said he would help me. And in case you didn't notice? People actually like him. They *want* to work with him, because he's not an arrogant jerk face."

Christopher looks around with fake curiosity. "Then where are the workers?"

"They're coming," I say through gritted teeth. There is a ball of fire inside me. It's an entire sun, its rays struggling to find a path out of my body. He doesn't give a fuck about me. About the library. So why is he so damn intent on ruining this?

"And in the meantime, you're... what? Living

here?"

"So what if I am? Maybe I camp out under the circulation desk with a sleeping bag. Maybe I use the antique books as kindling for more fire and eat roasted pigeons for dinner."

"What about your mother?" He says it as a challenge, which only serves to piss me off.

"What do you care about her? You didn't want her to have the treatment, and now she's not having it. The hospital doesn't get their expensive new butterfly garden. Happy now?"

"It's not safe here," he says flatly.

"Then why don't you leave?"

He turns away from me, and for a moment I think I'm going to see the back of him. It feels momentous, that his broad shoulders might walk away from me one last time. I don't know what my life would be like without his hard disdain. Without his censure. I long for the freedom as much as I ache for him to stay. One step. Two. He makes it six feet away before he stops.

I need him to hold me. To tell me everything will be okay.

"There's no way I can convince you to go?" He asks the question without looking at me.

He does worry about me, in that terrible white-knight kind of way. Terrible because it's how he keeps his distance. Like I'm someone he has to save instead of a woman he can hold. There's no life raft in this particular ocean, though. There's no saving me.

"Why did you come here?" I ask instead of answering.

Then he does face me. "I always come here. I can't seem to stop. It's the reason I bought this building, the reason why I planned to revitalize the west side."

"If you love the carving, why did you want to tear it down?"

A slight smile. "It's a bad habit of mine, destroying the things I love."

The word *love* coming from his mouth falls on me like a ton of bricks. The library walls falling on top of me couldn't hurt this much. My lungs burn from lack of air. Christopher Bardot has never loved anything. He's controlled and owned and protected—but never loved. Has he? He never cared about anything beyond ambition. Beyond money.

"Please," he murmurs, gentle as if he can sense my turmoil.

And Christopher Bardot has definitely never begged.

"I'm done for today," I say, my voice uneven.

It's hard to breathe in the face of this new side of him, still protective, still controlling, but somehow more real. Less like a stylized carving. More like a man who hurts and feels and wants. It makes me want to wrap myself in his arms, but what if he turns back into stone?

CHAPTER SIX

WORTH DOING WELL

I MET AVERY at Smith College, where she was the quintessential good student and I had a reputation as a wild child. It was easier to explain how I didn't know about a universal family tradition because I had been stuck in an Austrian boarding school. Easier to act unaffected by the infamy of my dysfunctional trust fund by pretending to obsess over parties and frat boys and reckless stunts.

It would be easier to really be as self-absorbed as people thought I was, but I felt every whisper, every criticism, every cruel smile directed at me as if my skin were made of paper.

I pull my leased BMW into the wide circular drive as the electronic gates swing open. Around back there's an eight-car garage with empty bays for Rolls-Royces and Aston Martins, the kind of cars befitting a house like this. I would have bought them, too, if Mom cared anything for cars.

Or if she could go anywhere.

"Helloooo," I call into the wide marble-floor foyer, hearing my voice echo back to me.

There's only silence.

I didn't feel guilty about the incident with that statue and the campus police. Those kinds of things were hobbies. Or maybe defense mechanisms. I didn't have the paralyzing doubt and self-recrimination I have now, when I dread coming home every evening.

Upstairs I find my mother napping even though it's already almost bedtime. She looks peaceful on her side, her hands resting one on top of the other. There would be no sign that she was unwell to someone who didn't know her. The main difference is her weight, something she's fought to keep down her entire life. Now she can't eat enough to even maintain her weight.

That's what the cancer does, takes all the nutrients away so her own cells starve.

It's her eyes that look the most different. There are dark shadows underneath her lashes. I can see the blue-green veins in her eyelids. They look sunken, especially when she opens them and smiles.

"There you are," she says, her voice rusty with sleep.

I brush her hair back, the way she did when I was a little girl. "Here I am. And I brought takeout."

She scrunches her nose. That's another side effect of the cancer. She doesn't even want to eat, when really her body needs even more calories. "I ate a big lunch."

"Well, you can have a little fried rice. And some sweet and sour chicken."

A disapproving sound. "There's some quinoa and kale salad in the fridge."

"I also got some fried wontons," I say in a singsong voice because no one can resist fried wontons—not even my mother. She's into whole grains and organic fruit, but they weren't enough to save her. Not even the herbalist or the acupuncture made a dent in the cancer.

She sits up, looking like some sleeping beauty awakened with a kiss. The irony is that if she'd done the rounds of chemo and experimental treatments that the doctor prescribed, she would look much worse. Her hair would be gone, her skin might be bruised.

And the cancer might have been held back, if

only for a few years.

I fought with her to do the treatments. Begged her. In the end it wasn't truly Christopher who kept her from having them. I had to accept that she didn't want that. That she wanted to live out what was left of her life with whatever peace she could find. This house is part of that peace. The fried wontons are part of that peace. But God, it hurts to watch it happen. It hurts bad enough that I dread coming home, and that's when I feel guilty.

"How's the library coming?"

She knows about the issues with contractors, though I haven't told her quite how dangerous it is for me to work on the restoration with the current structural problems. And I have no plans to tell her about Christopher Bardot, who's still a tender spot considering he left her destitute after taking the helm of my inheritance. I should not want a man who did that. I never should have been able to love him, in the deepest, most secret part of my heart. "The last shipment of oak looks really good. A close match. I'm going to stain it and see how it holds up. The bigger problem is my own skill with the chisel."

"You'll figure it out. I have faith in you."

I make a face. "Are you sure I shouldn't hire

someone? I talked to Professor Basu over e-mail, and she said there's a really promising woodworking artist who graduated last year."

She sits up, moving slowly because I know she gets dizzy sometimes. "I'm sure you'll do the right thing."

That's what she says when I'm thinking about doing the *wrong* thing. "The wall is worth doing well, even if I have to find someone else to do it."

"Someone else who understands your vision?"

That's the part that kept me from e-mailing Professor Basu back to ask for this guy's contact information. There's skill and there's passion. Both are required to do this wall. I don't have much skill in this medium, despite having graduated in studio art, but I don't trust anyone else to have the passion. The wall speaks to me, and with my clumsy hands I'm speaking back.

Mom stands up and then slides back to the bed. I catch her under her elbows, pulling her to standing. "Are you okay?" I breathe even though the answer is clearly no.

She's not okay. She's dying. That's what this house is—a personal hospice.

A place to say goodbye.

Her slender hand cups my cheek. "You're so strong," she whispers.

"I'm not," I whisper back because even now I want to fight her. I want to beg her to do some kind of therapy, even though I know we passed the point of no return. There's only death now, and waiting for it is killing me.

CHAPTER SEVEN

BUSINESS PARTNERS

I KNOW SOMETHING is different as I hopscotch over rubble.

A sharp mechanical sound cuts through the hum of male voices. The heavy plastic sheeting that protects the library from the elements is my very own looking glass. As I step through it, I find a whole bevy of strange creatures, muscled men with tools and boots, as if they stepped from the wall and became flesh.

They spare me a few glances, a little curious, mostly wary, before going about their work. It's almost noon, and though I only got up and showered an hour ago, the sheen of sweat on their brows tells me they've been at this a long time. They have hard hats on their heads and smudges on their dark shirts.

"Harper." The low voice makes me jolt.

I turn to face Sutton, who looks more like the old version of himself, the one I first met, wearing black slacks and a white button-down, the sleeves rolled up to reveal golden hair on his forearms. He isn't covered in smudges or sweat, but he does have a yellow hard hat on, burnished curls peeking out from beneath it.

My heart thumps a warm welcome for those forearms. "What are you doing here?"

"Restoring the library." He raises an eyebrow. "Like you asked me to."

"Well yeah, but I thought you couldn't find a construction crew willing to work on the library. And these people seem like they know what they're doing. Not like you found them on Craigslist."

"Thanks," he says drily. "They do know what they're doing, and I didn't find them on Craigslist. You don't need to worry about the library. How's your mother feeling?"

Guilt clenches my insides, along with worry and fear and a terrible grief that she's slipping through my fingers. I can't catch her. It's like reaching for smoke. "She's doing okay. How do you know she's in town?"

He lifts his shoulder in a vague shrug, which I assume means I wouldn't like his methods. A worker appears at his side to show him a paper. He scans it quickly, his blue eyes sharp, before nodding. The man hurries away to the next room where the books are kept.

"So what did you have to offer them?" I ask.

He steers me by my elbow away from the workers, his touch a delicate burn. "It occurred to me how strange it was for no one to take the job. Tanglewood isn't exactly in a construction boom right now, which is partly why we wanted to revitalize the west side."

"Christopher," I say grimly.

Blue eyes turn speculative. "How did you know that?"

I don't really want to tell him that Christopher was here last night—or that I was here, alone. "An educated guess. He's always been the meddling type."

"Meddling. That's one word for it. He hinted that they would get a big contract with his high-rise condos if they refused a renovation. It was rebuild or nothing, he told them."

"That bastard," I say faintly, hurt anew to hear it spelled out.

"Unfortunately he hinted that to every construction company. Once I convinced them of that, I had three bids on the table and more on the way if I waited for them to get their shit together."

"And you picked the lowest one?"

"Nope, I didn't go with any of those bids. Instead I brought in a company from Louisiana. Cost a pretty penny to transport the equipment and house the workers temporarily, but it's the principle of the thing. I'm sure you understand."

"That sounds like something Christopher would do."

A faint smile. "There's a reason we went into business together. If I'd let one of them take the job, they'd think they could get away with that next time. We deal honestly or not at all."

"Maybe Christopher was worried about our safety. About the safety of restoring the building now that the foundation has been compromised." The words ring false even as I say them, but admitting that Christopher screwed me over that completely still hurts.

Sutton gives me a droll look. "He's only worried about himself. It bothers him when the puppets don't dance on his strings."

There's a fist around my throat, making it hard to breathe. "You're probably right."

"Speaking of safety, I couldn't help but notice some loose carvings near the back. The wood is almost the same color, but they didn't come from the wall."

My cheeks heat. "Oh, I did a little work."

He takes off his hard hat with a knowing look and places it gently on my head. "You shouldn't be here without me. You shouldn't be here at all until the building is stabilized."

The yellow hard hat looked like a normal size on him, but it feels like an umbrella on my head, like I'm a little girl playing dress up. I peer up at him from beneath the brim. "This thing is heavy. How do you work with this on?"

"Only have to get hit with a falling chunk of concrete once before the hard hat looks appealing."

"There weren't any falling chunks of concrete last night, I promise."

He frowns. "But if there had been, if you had been injured, there would have been no one to help."

"That's not *quite* true." As soon as the words are out, I wish I could take them back. From the suspicion in Sutton's blue eyes he already knows what I have to say next. "Christopher came by."

He curses softly. "Of course he did. One of the construction companies probably gave him hell when I turned down their bid, which serves him right. God*damn* him."

Something warm and mysterious moves inside me, responding to the anger Sutton feels for Christopher. It's almost intimate, this fury. More like betrayal than a dissolved business partnership. It makes me wonder if they ever shared another woman. "Was it only me between you two?" I ask, hesitant. "Am I the only reason you resigned?"

A raised eyebrow. "Are you feeling guilty?"

"You're both big boys. I'm sure you can make your own decisions. I'm just curious."

He sighs, rubbing his hand at the back of his neck. "There was always some competition between us, but I'm pretty sure you could guess that. We're both ambitious."

"It's what helped you work well together," I guessed.

"It's what broke us apart in the end. You were part of it. Most of it, maybe. The physical side of it, but Bardot and Mayfair wouldn't have lasted even if you never came to town."

I have the sense of something beneath the surface, of watching a shadow move beneath a seemingly placid lake. "Why wouldn't the company have lasted?"

"Because it wasn't about the money," he says, his frustration almost tangible.

I hold my breath because I've wanted to hear those words forever. Wanted them to be real. Wanted something that wasn't about the money—but Sutton isn't talking about me right now. He's talking about Christopher Bardot while his deep inner turmoil vibrates through the air around us.

"What was it about?" I whisper, knowing he won't answer me.

The closed look on his face reminds me of Christopher. He can be just as cold and ruthless, even with his handsome golden-boy features, even with his easy charm. "It doesn't matter," he says finally. "The company is over. Dissolved after the library was purchased and the assets distributed."

I take a step closer, needing to know the answer. Feeling it at the tips of my fingers. Reaching for it. "Come to dinner with me, Sutton. We can go to L'Etoile again."

And we can fall on each other in a hallway. He can lift my couture skirt and make me see stars. It doesn't matter what restaurant we go to. That's how the night would end.

His blue eyes turn dark. I don't mistake the desire. "We're business partners. That's it."

"The way you and Christopher were business partners?"

Something flashes across his face. "Yes," he says. "Like that."

"Then we can meet where you met him. At the Den, for cognac or whiskey or whatever the hell rich men like to drink these days. We work together now. You don't have an excuse."

There's every chance tonight will end the same way.

He stares me down, willing me to look away first. Except I want this too much. I want *him* too much, in all his conflicted glory, even if he is some kind of consolation prize. Even if that's what I am for him. He courted me once, and he was damn charming then. But now he's resisting me, trying to be reserved, and he's damn near devastating.

I might be the one falling to my knees in front of him tonight.

"Beer," he says, his voice rough. "At the Den. Nine o'clock."

I take off the yellow hard hat and hold it out to him. "You need this more than me. I don't want any wayward pieces of concrete knocking you out. I'm pretty sure they don't serve beer in the ER."

He gives me a small smile, but it doesn't reach his eyes.

I'm still wondering about that look as I step back through the heavy plastic sheeting, as I cross back through the looking glass into the real world of traffic horns and exhaust.

The way you and Christopher were business partners? There was something in his expression when I asked the question. Guilt. Longing?

It makes me wonder if there was more to their relationship than money. It makes me wonder if I broke more than their company when I stood between them.

CHAPTER EIGHT

NATURAL PART OF LIFE

M Y MOTHER'S NURSE is a stout woman with perpetually pink cheeks and a tendency to call everyone *sugar*. Freida dutifully prepares the chopped kale salads and wheatgrass smoothies my mother prefers, but I suspect she laces the brownies with pot.

Whatever we're paying the agency, it isn't enough.

I like her so much I can almost forget that she isn't a regular nurse. She's a hospice nurse, part of a whole hospice team that consulted with my mother for weeks when we moved here.

Daddy died in the middle of my first art gallery show, to the shock of everyone.

What came after, the will and its humiliation, that was a surprise, too.

My mother seems determined to die in exactly

the opposite way—slowly, with every stage planned out. I'm sure it comes from a kindness, a wish to prevent the kind of paralysis that gripped us in that New York City hotel room, the air still tinged with the smell of paint.

Freida manages to corner me. I'm usually more careful than this, but I sneaked into the kitchen for a pot brownie and a glass of milk. I could have used a little natural high before seeing Sutton in his natural element. There's nothing behind me except a walk-in pantry, no possible escape from the conversation I've been avoiding for almost a month.

"Harper," she says. "I'm glad I caught you, sugar."

I wave the plate with the pot brownie vaguely, as if I'm not panicking inside. "Oh, you know, just getting a midnight snack. It's something I do when I'm sleepwalking. Like right now."

She gives me that hospice-nurse smile. "We should talk about your mother."

"You already told me what she ate today," I say as if she's just so silly. As if there's nothing else to say about a woman determined to die in the most drawn-out possible way.

"We should talk about the Death Plan, Harper."

And there it is.

I still can't believe there's something even called a Death Plan. Who plans for death? It's the worst possible outcome, and even if it's inevitable, even if you see it coming, how can you accept it with something as terrible as Times New Roman printed on cheap inkjet paper?

"I really don't think I need to talk about it, actually. Bad enough that it exists."

She doesn't move out of my way. "The purpose is to make the event easier for you."

"Easier? Death isn't supposed to be easy."

"Maybe not easy, but it doesn't have to be hard. Death is a natural part of life."

God. Is that what the Death Plan says? Ten thousand percent glad I haven't read it. "I know Mom was into this whole hospice, kumbaya, circle-of-life thing, and I respect that, but that doesn't mean I have to join the club. No leather jacket for me, okay?"

"She would really like you to be on the same page."

No, it's not respecting her wishes, but I can't read that sheet of paper any more than I can stab my eyes with a steak knife. That's actually looking more and more like a reasonable exit as Freida continues to stand in front of the door to the kitchen.

It may not look like much, but I'm doing the best I can. I'm not fighting for my mother to continue treatment. I'm not begging doctors for favors or circling the world for a new experimental medicine. I'm here to face her death, but I don't have to read the script.

"You can't avoid this forever," she says gently.

"Watch me."

It strikes me how this is the opposite of Daddy's death. His will was a secret when he died, taking all of us by surprise. Maybe even him. Instead there's an actual plan for Mom's death. There won't be any surprises, any pain, because dying is just a part of life, right? Unless the paper says, *Just kidding, I'm not dying,* there's nothing that can make this easier.

The nurse takes a step back, giving me enough room to squeeze by. "My job isn't only to care for the dying. I'm here to help the family, too."

I stare at her, more bemused than frustrated. "Does that ever actually work?"

She pauses for only a moment. "I hope so."

And I think I'm not the only woman trying to turn straw into gold. I'm not the only woman failing. There are a million impossible tasks we give ourselves, trapped in a room with no way out. Part of me wants to throw my arms around Freida and sob into her warmth. Instead I leave the brownie on the counter and go upstairs to change into something sexy and ill-advised. It's going to take something a lot stronger to make me forget tonight.

CHAPTER NINE

SELF DESTRUCT

THE DEN IS part gentleman's club, where socializing happens with liquor and cigars. Part Renaissance salon, where ideas are discussed. And part boardroom, where deals are made.

Both Sutton and Christopher are regulars here, which means I put on my best dress. Even Mom notices the effort, telling me I'll turn heads tonight. I might not be with either man right now, but I can at least show them what they're missing. Tonight I need something that shallow. Something that selfish. Something that sweet.

Tonight that means a strapless red gown that flares into an asymmetrical sweep beside my knee. It's head-turning anywhere, but in the low lamp glow of the Den I'm like a walking, talking beacon to the men around me. There are a hundred eyes on my body as I weave around crinkled leather chairs and thick wood stools.

The first person I recognize is Blue, a man I've met here before who runs a security company. He's standing at the bar, watching the men who watch me. There's definitely no Sutton, no lazy smile as he waits for me and that drink. Unease curls through my stomach. Did he stand me up?

"Whatever's on tap," I tell the bartender, sliding across a twenty.

An assortment of gold and clear liquids line mirrored shelves behind the bar, but I find myself craving the cool froth of a beer. Maybe it was hearing Sutton say the word, that it somehow eroticized an otherwise ordinary drink. He has that effect on more than beverages—the heat of morning across my cheeks, the metal scent of the earth.

All of it becomes the backdrop to his elemental charisma.

A large glass of amber beer appears in front of me, the glass already condensing.

Blue slides the bill back to me. "It's on me. The least I can do considering I earned many times that spying on you. What makes you so intriguing, Ms. St. Claire?"

So that's how Christopher knew about my mother. "I'm sure I have no idea. It must be really boring to watch me read books and pick up Thai food."

"I don't watch you personally, but I see the reports."

That makes me snort. "'She ordered the yellow curry today instead of the red.'"

"Interesting enough that I can sell it to more than one entity."

That must mean Sutton is paying for information, too. And why not? Both he and Christopher are friends with Blue Eastman. That's how I met him. It doesn't have to bother me that they're both nosy and manipulative. It doesn't have to hurt.

The ache in my heart proves me wrong.

My gaze scans the room back and forth, back and forth. Only when my heart leaps do I realize I'm not looking for sky-blue eyes and blond hair. Not only that. I'm keeping an eye out for Christopher, unable to keep myself from hoping. That will go on my tombstone, I'm sure of it— *here lies Harper St. Claire, unable to keep herself from hoping.*

"Shouldn't you be at home changing diapers?" I ask.

Blue nods toward a closed velvet curtain. "I would, but I'm on the clock. We have two clients in the game. They both have their own body-guards, but I figured I'd better check in."

"The game?"

"Poker," he clarifies.

"Does that often get violent?"

"All the men around the table are armed." At my shudder he adds, "Not everyone who works for me can get the cushy job of tailing little girls to the library."

I scrunch my nose. "I'm not a little girl. And I don't need a bodyguard."

"That's good because he's not there to guard you. Look at it this way—at least if the building comes down on you, there will be someone to dial 9-1-1."

"He won't come in after me?"

A faint smile. "He has orders not to engage."

"Cold," I say, but I can't help laughing. "At least show me pictures."

He looks only too glad to pull out his phone. A quick swipe reveals a chubby-cheeked baby with her eyes closed tight, tucked into the arms of a woman I recognize as Blue's young wife. "She's twelve weeks."

"She's so beautiful, both of them."

He scrolls to the left, where a wide-eyed tod-dler offers a biscuit to the infant. Another one where a large golden dog sniffs the baby, who wears footie pajamas. Then there's a little girl with chestnut curls riding a pony, wearing a tiara and rainbow leggings.

"Three of them?" I ask, raising my eyebrows.

"And they're all as beautiful as their mother." He keeps scrolling through an endless display of familial love, and I soak it up. Until another swipe reveals a woman who must be his wife. They're in a fancy restaurant with china and wineglasses between them. Date night? She's looking up, a little shy, a mild reproach, as if he's snapping a picture against her wishes.

"She *is* beautiful," I admit, my voice solemn. "What did she see in you?"

He gives me a secret smile. "I didn't give her much choice."

The words might be ominous if I hadn't seen such love glowing from the dark eyes in the photo. "A husband who actually wants to stay with his wife. A little strange where I come from."

Blue tucks his phone back in his pocket. "And where is it that you come from?"

"I'm surprised that's not in your fancy reports." It probably is, but I humor him anyway. "I suppose you could say I come from all over the place. All over the country. All over the world.

But mostly you could say I come from money."

He nods. "That's a whole different ball game."

I take in his tailored suit, which molds to his large body perfectly. The watch that easily rivals something the fancy businessmen in the Den are wearing. "I think you play that game just fine."

"It helps when you're so damn entertaining you have half the Tanglewood population paying for information about you. If you get any more interesting, I'll be able to buy a vacation home."

On that note he gives me a small salute and walks toward the velvet curtains. I slip inside after him, pretending I have every right to be here. It takes a second to adjust to the dim light and smoke in the air. Then I see players sitting around the table and someone dressed in a white dress shirt and a maroon vest that must be the dealer.

There's Damon Scott, leaning back like a king in his three-piece suit, which is a reasonable analogy considering he owns the Den. His fingers drum against cards facedown on the table.

Beside him is a man I don't recognize, with deeply tanned skin and dark hair in wild disarray, his eyes a striking green. A man who can only be a bodyguard stands beside him, filling out his suit almost to bursting, his jaw hard-set. As I watch, Blue joins him and murmurs something.

Then there's Christopher Bardot, who scans the cards he holds with pure calculation. I don't really know what counting cards entails, but I'm sure he's doing it. Not as part of any trick, but because his analytical, highly intelligent brain can't help but solve the equation on the velvet table.

He looks up, his black eyes widening in surprise. "Harper," he says, his voice low. Somehow intimate even as we sit in a roomful of people.

On the other side of the table are more men I don't recognize, one young and determined, the other weathered and shrewd, both with a smaller pile of chips. A bodyguard stands behind a gorgeous woman with dark hair who has a large pile of chips.

And then there's Sutton, sitting directly across from Christopher. He leans back, deceptively casual in his seat. He doesn't look like a man about to meet me for a drink. I think he would have spent the whole night in here.

From across the room he catches my gaze. His blue eyes are wide as the sky above Gold Rush, leading me toward a horizon I'll never reach. He looks at me with both desire and determination, as if he's pushing me away. As if he wants me to choose Christopher. I'm about two seconds away from breaking completely, and these men are playing games. It makes me want to hurt him, even if it means hurting myself.

Sutton watches me with opaque blue eyes, his expression unreadable. It isn't exactly welcoming, but I feel my body open to him anyway. To the warmth he emanates like a goddamn sun. One step, two. My hips sway to a rhythm only I can hear, and I feel some of my old confidence return. This is the Harper St. Claire wanted by every frat boy—and some of the sorority girls, too. This is the Harper St. Claire who owns the room.

This is Harper St. Claire, pressing the self-destruct button.

I'll break into a million pieces, but I'll take them all with me.

I don't bother with anything so mundane as permission. I don't wait for him to welcome me. Instead I throw myself into his lap, and he doesn't miss a beat.

As if my body is made to fall. As if his is made to catch me.

Up close I can see the glint of bristle on his jaw, the tired lines under his eyes. Why is he playing a high-stakes game when he's tired? A surge of affection takes me by surprise. Lust is something I understand. With a man built like him it's only natural. I run my fingers through his golden hair, yanking a little before I let him go.

The corner of his mouth quirks up. "You want to play, Harper?"

There's a pull deep inside my body, an answering *yes* that comes from the memory of how it can be between us. Hot. Intense. Devastating. "I'm just here to watch."

A small smile. "Then watch."

The words sound unbearably erotic, as if I'm going to watch something more intimate than a high-stakes poker game. I turn slightly in Sutton's lap so that I can see the table. And his cards. I touch them with my forefinger, affecting a surprised look. "Hey, there's one of these on the table!"

Sounds of muffled amusement come from around the table. The man with dark tousled hair gives a bark of laughter. "Watch your woman, Mayfair," he says with a curl of his lip.

"She doesn't belong to him," Christopher says, his voice sharp.

Something flashes through his onyx eyes, something I've never seen there—violence. It's cold and calculating, everything I know him to be. And terribly serious. I'm not sure whether he's mad that the stranger's words implied ownership—or that he said I belonged to Sutton instead of him.

An uneasy silence descends on the table, which makes me flutter my eyelashes at the stranger. "I'm sorry, I don't think we've been introduced. I'm Harper. Harper St. Claire."

"Ms. St. Claire," the man says with a look I suppose some women would find charming. It reminds me of a snake, the way it studies you before striking. "Your reputation precedes you."

Sutton tenses. The words would be a compliment to a man. They're the worst kind of insult to a woman. "You want to be careful," he says softly, mirroring the earlier warning.

The man grins, looking like the dictionary entry for *reckless*. "I meant her artwork, of course. And her social causes. What was it you wanted to free? A post office?"

Asshole. "It was a library. And you are?"

He manages a small, mocking bow while remaining seated. "Victor Emmanuel, Prince of Piedmont. At your service, of course."

"A prince." I give a wide-eyed look. "Is that like Prince Harry? Are you going to marry a commoner? Oh, I do love a royal wedding."

That earns me a lazy smile. "I suppose I haven't met the right woman."

The statement could be considered flirting if he hadn't basically just called me a slut in a roomful of people. Does he think he could get away with that because he's minor royalty? I can feel Christopher's anger in the air, feel Sutton's tension beneath me. From the corner of my eyes I see Blue and his bodyguards stiffen, as if preparing for a fight to break out.

What was it Blue said? All the men around the table are armed. Oh God.

"We're here to play cards," Damon says, gently chiding. He runs the Den and makes plenty of money off these games. I suppose it wouldn't help to have bloodshed. He tosses his cards in. "And I'm out."

"That's probably for the best," I tell him in my innocent voice. I glance at Sutton's hand again. "His cards are really good. I mean *really* good."

Damon only smirks back at me, probably seeing right through the act. Because Sutton's hand really is good, but it's not the one pair that I implied when I first sat down. No, he's got a flush with a queen high. And I'm playing this clueless act to get someone to stay in, thinking they can beat him when they can't.

Victor the Asshole Prince, that's what I'm

going to call him. He winks at me before tossing in a thousand-dollar marker. "Raise," he says pleasantly.

Christopher's eyes sear me from across the table. I know for sure he sees through my ruse, which means he knows that Sutton's cards must be actually good. Then he narrows his gaze on my hip, where I feel the warmth of a large hand, where the calluses must surely catch on the silk of my dress. My whole body seems to turn inside out, as if I'm naked for the table. He tosses his cards into the pile. "Fold."

The last of the players hem and haw over the increased amount, but in the end they stack up hundred-dollar chips and push them into the pile, where they topple over.

I clap my hands. "Your turn."

Sutton's breath is warm against my cheek. "Dangerous," he murmurs.

Maybe he means the Asshole Prince, who's bound to be angry that he's just lost a thousand dollars—more counting his ante and earlier bids. Or maybe he means the dance that's happening between our bodies, the push and pull, the sensual conversation that doesn't need a word.

I'm the one who picks up two chips that say *$500* on them and tosses them on the pile. Then I flip over his cards and point at them idly, letting my fingers trail over the diamonds that match the ones faceup on the table. "This is called something, right?"

Damon gives a low laugh. "It's called playing poker, darling. And you do it well."

Asshole Prince swears rather creatively, which is the most interesting thing he's said since I got here. He tosses his cards onto the table, revealing three of a kind. Not bad. The other players throw their cards on the table. A pair of kings—lame. And a low straight which isn't bad but still isn't enough to win.

Christopher doesn't crack a smile, but I feel his amusement. It burns as hot as Sutton's body beneath me, behind me, around me—making me feel like I'm being embraced from all sides.

I clap and bounce on Sutton's lap, making him grunt. "Oooh, you won all these chips?"

As I stand up to pull the chips toward me, I dip low enough to show my cleavage. There are many nice cleavages in the world, but this one is mine. And I don't mind showing Asshole Prince what he's missing. Except it isn't the wild, reckless eyes I meet, but Christopher's calculating ones. He saw right through my little ruse. And as I pull back the chips, I have the strange sensation that he's seeing right through me.

I sit back down with a sudden thump, and Sutton's hands grasp my hips hard enough to make me gasp. There's something else hard down there; an erection that presses against my dress. Oh God, I'd shoved my ass into his face when I gathered the chips. I make neat little piles with them, focusing hard so that I don't have to look at Christopher or acknowledge the arousal of the man holding me.

Asshole Prince stands and places his hands flat on the table, and it feels like he's looming over me even though there's a table between us and three armed bodyguards around us. "You must think you're clever, little girl?"

"I think she's clever," Damon Scott says, sounding amused.

"She does like to watch," Asshole Prince says, mischief entering his dark eyes. "She lines up the little matchstick men and then lights us on fire."

"That's poetic," I say archly. "If a little gruesome."

"I'm sure we'll meet again," he says, giving me a real bow this time. "For now I'm afraid I must take my chips and my bruised ego and live to play another day."

His departure seems to signal the end of the

game. The other players leave, including Damon, who says in a drawl that we can use the room for as long as we like. It makes me wonder how many dirty things have happened in this velvet-curtained space.

Then it's only Christopher and Sutton. And me.

This is the part where I'm supposed to stand up and walk away. This is the part where I prove to these men—and to myself—that I can be the girl I was before. That I didn't shatter into a million pieces, suspended in the air, about to fall.

Instead I whisper, "I don't want to go home."

It's an admission. A confession to the two men who can most use it against me. There is no home for me anymore. There's only hospice and Death Plan and the longest goodbye.

CHAPTER TEN

ONE PERCENTER

SUTTON KNOWS WHAT the problem is immediately. I can sense it in the way he embraces me, the way it turns from seductive to comforting, the way he seems to almost let me go. "Harper," he says gently. "You're so strong. It's okay to need a break."

"I want more than a break," I say, full of grim, self-recriminating guilt.

It takes me twenty minutes with my eyes squeezed tight, building myself to act normal, act natural, before I can even walk into a room with her. And another twenty minutes muffling my tears into a pillow after I leave. I need one night with these men, because I know they can distract me. Even if they break my heart afterward.

He turns my hand over and threads his fingers through mine. "You can lean on us."

Christopher leans back across the table. "Lean on us?"

"Yes," Sutton says, his voice lower now. "We can help her through this."

"I'm planning on it." Christopher gives me a dark stare. "She didn't come here looking for a shoulder to cry on. For that she would have gone to her friends."

Sutton gives a mocking laugh. "As if you know anything about friendship."

"I don't." A shrug. "But she didn't wear *that* dress to talk."

A stroke down my side, over the smooth red silk of my dress. Sutton must feel that I'm not wearing a bra. Or panties. He must sense the truth in Christopher's words. Even if I told myself I only wanted to talk to Sutton, my body knew the truth. I came here to forget.

"Is that true?" Sutton murmurs against my neck, soft enough so only I can hear. "Do you want this? Because if you don't, I can make him leave. I can take you home. Whatever you need."

"What if I don't know what that is?" I whisper.

Christopher stands with an animal grace. "Pretend you don't want this, if it helps. That goes for the both of you. I'll be the villain in this story."

Every muscle in my body pulls taut as Christopher rounds the table. Sutton holds me tighter, almost painfully. I know he'd protect me if I wanted him to. I could probably cause a fistfight right now, and there's a kind of power in that. Except maybe Christopher is right.

Maybe I want the power taken away from me tonight.

"Her wrists," Christopher says, all lazy command. "Hold them."

Sutton shifts like he might protest, like he might object to holding me in bondage, or maybe he'd only mind Christopher being the one to call the shots. Last time there were three of us in a room like this, it had been Sutton who gave the orders. Sutton who taunted the other man. He'd held me much like this, standing instead of sitting, my body between them, but he had been the one to give orders.

Large hands close around my wrists, and my eyelids flutter closed. A small sound escapes me, maybe from nerves, maybe relief. I'm already on display on Sutton's lap. Having my hands behind my back makes it worse. My breasts push against the silk, the folds of my red skirt spilling over Sutton's black slacks, a startling contrast. I have to pull my arms, only a little, to see if I can get away.

"You like this?" Sutton murmurs. "I know you can feel me. You like making me so hard for you? You love having two men panting after you?"

They're not really panting, though.

Christopher looks at me the same way he looked at the poker table. Like he's counting all the cards, effortless, almost clinical. And Sutton makes me feel small and delicate the way he holds me so gently, using only one percent of the muscle mass in his body to keep me still.

"She loves it," Christopher says, his voice hard as a diamond.

Sutton moves my wrists to his left hand, freeing his right to smooth across my hip. Down my thigh. Between my legs. There are miles of fabric between him and my sex, but it burns up into nothing. It's as if those calloused hands are brushing right over my clit, the way it feels. His hand looks rough and dark against the expensive silk.

"Where do you want it?" he asks, cupping me through the dress. "Here?"

"Oh God," I mumble, barely resisting the urge to push into his hand.

Two laughs, masculine and goddamn confident. They know exactly what they're doing to me. Christopher takes a step closer, so he's standing only a foot away. Close enough that I can see the rumple in his dress shirt, the invisible scar at the top of his lip. Close enough that I can smell him, the spice and maleness. And arousal. I'm not sure if arousal has a smell, but if it does, we're awash in it. We're an ocean of desire, the three of us.

The silk gathers around my breasts in complicated folds. Christopher runs the back of his hand down my front, making it simple. My nipples turn hard and aching. Then he slips one finger beneath the neckline. He's only touching an extra inch of skin, one inch that isn't showing, but it feels momentous. Like crossing the Rubicon.

He adds another finger, brushing the skin at my collarbone back and forth. He can't quite reach my nipple like this, and my body tightens everywhere, as if I can make him touch me by will alone.

"Let me look at her," Christopher says, and I'm not sure exactly what he means until I feel Sutton's knuckles against my back, until I hear the rasp of the delicate zipper.

The bodice falls away from my body, leaving a shadow.

Christopher tugs the dress away from me,

revealing my upthrust breasts, my pink nipples. His swift intake of breath is a small comfort. This is affecting him as much as me.

"Are you okay?" Sutton asks, and it's more than a question. It's an escape. That's what he's offering me. All I have to do is say the word and he'll zip up my dress. He'll probably drive me home.

Christopher lifts my chin, forcing me to meet his dark gaze. "What do you want?"

It's the same question, wrapped in different packaging.

What do I want? I want to go back in time, before I ever met Sutton or Christopher. I want to be the kind of woman who doesn't fall in love. I want the world to be a place where men don't leave and mothers don't die, but I can't say those things. They aren't the kind of sexy answers that make sense when two handsome men are surrounding you, their bodies taut with desire. They used to be partners, these men. Not anymore.

"Both of you," I manage to say, my voice a wisp of smoke.

That earns me a smile, a cruel kind of smile. "Then spread your legs for Sutton. He's going to finger fuck you while I play with your tits."

The words come harsh enough that I expect Sutton to balk. Except his cock pulses beneath my ass. His hand tightens around my wrists. And I have the sudden awareness that he likes Christopher being in charge—not only of me, but of both of us. That maybe his taunting control in the hotel room six months ago had been an act designed to protect him, as much as my obedience is supposed to protect me.

I don't quite spread my legs, but I don't fight when Sutton pulls my thigh open. His large hand gathers up my skirt with steady deliberation, folds and folds of it, continents of fabric, the anticipation making me wet more than his hand could do. At least that's how it seems. Until he touches me, the large clasp of his hand holding my sex a jolt to my system.

I gasp, fighting the hold at my wrists for a second before I subside. "You're such an asshole," I say, my voice breaking when Sutton slides his blunt fingertips through my wetness.

Christopher smiles. "Keep going."

One finger inside me. Two. *Oh God.* "You bastard. You prick. You're the worst kind of arrogant, entitled, one percenter, first-world problems, my-iPhone-is-too-slow, do-you-know-who-I-am, goddamn designer-suit-wearing asshole."

He runs a thumb over my lips, making me shiver. "It's going to feel so good to fuck this mouth. And what's wrong with my suits?"

They're beautiful. Everything about him is cold and beautiful. "I hate you."

His thumb pushes into my mouth. "So fucking good."

"If you want me to bite you."

He looks unconcerned. "Do you want to fuck her?" he asks Sutton, without taking his dark gaze off my lips. "I think she's about ready. Past ready, to be honest. Practically begging for it."

Sutton places a kiss on the side of my neck, his tenderness a contrast to Christopher. He moves higher, his lips firm. And higher, to the sensitive space beneath my ear. His teeth gently tug my lobe. "Ask me to fuck you, sweetheart. I want to hear you say it."

I let my head fall back to Sutton's shoulder. "Please."

"The words," he says, his voice gentle but uncompromising.

"I want you to... to fuck me. Oh God. Please, Sutton."

"Why do you want me to fuck you?" he asks, his voice terribly gentle, and in that moment I hate him as much as I hate Christopher. More, because he actually has a heart in that broad chest.

"Because I'm..." His thumb circles my clit, around and around, never hard enough to help. "I'm so turned on, and it's hurting, and I want you. And God, I'm so empty. And I'm broken." The honesty slips through the millions of cracks around me. "I'm barely holding it together."

That must be what they wanted, all the pain inside me, because Sutton reaches between us to undo his pants. Christopher produces a condom for him, as if this is well coordinated. They work together to keep my hands behind my back while Sutton sheathes himself. He nudges against me, still covered by the galaxy of my dress. And then he's pushing inside, impossibly large. Maybe it's the angle we're using, or the fact that it's been six months since I was with them, but the stretch makes me gasp. My eyes prick with pain I can't quite hide.

"Wait," Christopher says, proving that maybe he does care.

"Fuck," Suttons says, his voice strained. "Can't." He pushes deeper, making my hips jerk. His hands are like iron against my legs. "She's so tight. Too tight. You need to help her."

Christopher is pushing aside his clothes, revealing a cock large and throbbing. Almost painful looking, the way it's reddened. The way it's wet at the tip. He places the slick head against my lips. "Open."

This isn't the kind of help Sutton meant—or maybe it is. My eyes are wide as I stare up at him. Wide and mutinous. I'm not going to give in easy, not when it feels like I'm being split underneath.

A pinch to my nipple makes me gasp, and then his cock slides along my tongue. Oh God, I'm doing this. It's not anything like what I imagined a blowjob would be. There's no licking or sucking. Instead I'm immobile while his hips move him deep into my mouth, the head butting against my throat. I make a gagging sound, and he pulls back. "Jesus," Christopher says, and it sounds like an imprecation. A prayer.

This is what I asked for, isn't it? Begging for it, that's what Christopher said, but I could never have imagined this. The strain of it. The fullness that laps against pain like an ocean on the shore.

In a way I did ask for this, because I wanted to forget. There was something that bothered me, but I can't possibly remember it now. It ceases to exist in the face of this raw physicality.

"Not going to last," Sutton says on a grunt.

Christopher pushes forward, and I can't help

the gag reflex. He pulls out, and I feel my tongue slide along the slit of his cock as I take in air. His eyes glaze with pleasure. This is the weakest I've ever seen him, and he's mesmerizing like this. Is this how I look to them with my hands behind my back? He looks like he belongs to me, pushing back into my mouth like he can't imagine leaving.

Then he does something he's never done before. He puts his hand on Sutton's shoulder. To support himself as he struggles with the pleasure of a blowjob? A gesture of camaraderie as they fuck the same woman? I don't know what it means, but it's the most intimate thing that's happened between us.

Sutton goes rock-hard beneath me. His cock flexes. His hands tighten, and then he's groaning his release. He shouts it into my hair, against my skin, biting the place where my shoulder meets my neck.

In his climax he pinches my clit, and I'm coming, biting down on nothing because there's no cock in my mouth, clenching hard around a thick cock, feeling rivulets of my arousal slide down my thighs.

Christopher jerks himself in front of me, hard, punishing, twisting at the end until he throws his head back and comes in a warm spray across my chin, my collarbone, my dress.

CHAPTER ELEVEN

FOR THE BEST

I'M STILL PANTING when Sutton gently sets me down on the cushioned chair, the fabric still warm from his body. He straightens his clothes, his hands shaking only a little.

Christopher produces a monogrammed hand-kerchief from the pocket of his suit and uses it to wipe my skin clean, but I can still feel him there. I'm branded with his arousal, and with mine. "I'll get you something to drink," he says, leaving me alone with the man I was supposed to have drinks with. The man who basically stood me up and got laid for it.

Only he looks more messed up by the whole thing than me.

Those strong hands tamed a wild horse, but they don't look steady now. Sutton can't quite meet my eyes as he moves a poker chip between his fingers and knocks it against the table. For good luck? Except the game is already over.

"I can't do this," he says, his voice hoarse.

"It's already done." I'm still feeling sore and stretched from where his large cock impaled me. Feeling raw that Sutton would reject me one second after he leaves my body. He was supposed to be the man I could choose. The one who chose me. Instead he seems more shaken than Christopher about what just happened. "And it sure seemed like you enjoyed yourself."

That earns me a dark laugh. "Yes, the way an insect enjoys the silk of a spider's web."

I raise my eyebrows. "Am I the spider in this story?"

His blue gaze takes me in from head to disheveled toe. "You're the web."

"God." There's enough strength left in my body to stand. "You want to act helpless? You want to play games with a billion dollars from my trust fund and then fuck me and then act like you're the one who's hurt? Go to hell, Sutton."

"Already there," he says, and the way his eyes burn, I believe it.

He turns and leaves me standing beside the poker table, alone in a room that was filled with men when I entered. That's how I can clear a room, ladies and gentlemen. Welcome to the Harper St. Claire show. I collapse back into the chair and rest my head on the back. There's a hollow in my chest, but I can't even blame it on Sutton for leaving. I can't blame it on Christopher for staying. It comes from deep inside, to the place that no man can fill. The sex only numbed me for so long. Grief comes rushing back in to fill the void, acid in my throat.

Footsteps approach.

A glass of dark red wine is placed in front of me. Christopher throws back a shot of clear liquid—probably vodka. There isn't a third glass. "What about Sutton?"

Dark eyes study me. "I'm sure he can get a drink wherever he's gone."

"Shouldn't you go talk to him or something? You were partners."

"We were partners. Now we're nothing." A shrug, all the more hurtful because of how casual he seems. "You didn't expect him to stick around, did you?"

"I kind of… did. Yes." What's the etiquette for a backroom threesome?

Christopher sighs as if I'm terribly naive. "What we did here… it isn't going to last."

That makes me laugh, sharp and breathless.

Because it's been a long time since I was naive. "You mean you're not going to marry me with an ironclad prenup and then divorce me in a year so that we can spend the rest of our lives hating each other? I'm shocked."

A quirk of his lips. "Not every man is your dad, Harper."

"And not every woman is your mother. Why do you think I expect anything permanent? Because I'd like someone to say goodbye after... after..."

"Sex," he says gently.

I hate the look in his eyes, almost like pity. It was better when he stared down at me like he was going to devour me. Better when he snapped and snarled at me from across the poker table. "After sex," I repeat, only a little broken. "Isn't that what normal people do?"

"I have no idea what normal people do, but I don't think Sutton is anything near normal. Oh, he may have fooled you with that Southern boy act, but he's as fucked-up as any of us. More."

"You would say that," I say, though I sense the truth of his words. The weight of them.

"I've seen Sutton date a lot of women. Charm them. Make them fall in love. He doesn't stick around. At least I'm honest about it. I've never promised anything to a woman."

"Never promise anything, never let them down, right?"

"Is that wrong?"

"No, it's perfectly right." I'm unable to hide the hurt. "Christopher Bardot, always doing the most correct thing. A-plus on your Honesty in Sexual Relations exam. The model student."

His eyes flash at my tone. "I'm going to drive you home now."

As if I would take a ride from him. He was burning for me only thirty minutes ago. Now he's so cold I'm practically shivering. I would probably freeze to death by the time we got there. "No, thanks."

"Don't be difficult."

"Difficult. *Difficult?* Oh, you haven't seen difficult yet."

"Goddamn it, Harper. Would it kill you to do what I say once in a while?"

"I might listen to you if I thought you actually gave a damn. Sutton told me what you did, keeping all the construction crews away from us."

"That was for your own good."

My laugh feels like acid in my throat. "Right."

"I know you're upset," he says in an overly reasonable tone. "You're under a lot of stress right now. Do you need more help at home? I can speak with the service."

I want to set him on fire with my eyes. "Now you want to help? When my mother struggled for so long, so many years, that you could have made easier? Because it took her getting cancer before you let me control the fucking trust fund?"

He could be made of stone, this granite statue planted in front of me, eternal and unfeeling. "The money doesn't help?"

The money... God, the money. I would burn it all to the ground.

Some speck of sanity remains inside me, because I know that wouldn't help anyone. "No, the money doesn't help when cancer cells are eating her alive, when they're starving her from the inside, and she refuses medical treatment."

He looks at me with his onyx eyes, and I think he might actually say something human. Something like the Christopher Bardot I met years ago on my father's yacht. It would devastate me, to see kindness from him. It would give me hope.

A lift of his shoulder. "It's probably for the best."

"For the best? It's for the best that she isn't letting the doctors help her. They have new treatments, advances in medicine." My voice rises, and I know I sound crazy. I *feel* crazy. Maybe it was foolish to expect kindness from this man, but this coldness is a new level. "How can her dying be for the best? Tell me that, Christopher."

"Better that she goes sooner than prolong it."

He should not be able to shock me. I know every dark angle inside Christopher Bardot. I know better than to expect anything like compassion from him, but God, I'm stunned. My mouth is open. No words come out. There's only silence for an endless moment.

"I hate you," I whisper. And it's not a sexy blowjob kind of hate.

It's a bone-deep grief.

I don't want wine, but I take a sip anyway, letting the acid wash away any lingering taste of him. The first sob takes me by surprise. It's loud, filling a room made for excess and pleasure. The second one I capture with my hands, shaking with the force of it. Sorrow isn't a quiet thing; it's an earthquake inside me. It takes over until I'm breaking apart, sitting still, trying to catch my tears and failing.

Someone appears in front of me. A large hand on my shoulder.

Then I'm wrapped in strong arms and lifted.

It could be anyone taking me anywhere.

Christopher taking me home—finally, finally. That terrible prince taking me to the depths of hell, for all I know, but I press my face into the broad chest. The linen becomes soaked immediately, cold against my skin from tears that are hot on my cheeks. One long sob that I can feel in the base of my throat, and I suck in air, breathing in the earthy scent of Sutton.

Thick night air. The smell of exhaust. The muted sound of a car door, and then I'm in the back of a limo, still ensconced in Sutton's arms. He doesn't try to stop me from crying.

"You left," I finally manage to say, my voice heavy with tears. Drenched with them.

He holds me a little tighter. "I came back."

CHAPTER TWELVE

MILK AND COOKIES

FREIDA IS KIND enough to pretend like it's ordinary to arrive home completely disheveled, my dress stained with something mysterious, my eyes red and puffy from crying. She gives me the information for the evening, what my mother ate, what she *didn't* eat, with a completely straight face—which is all the more impressive when I actually look in the mirror.

"I really have to shower first," I say with a groan. Mascara has made track marks down my cheeks. I look like a girl in a horror movie who's been running for her life and about to die. "She'll call the police if she sees me like this. You can go home now."

Sutton shakes his head. He doesn't seem himself, not quite as assured, but he looks very certain about this. "I'm staying until you go to bed."

I give him a sideways look. "You hoping for a round two?"

A faint smile. "Always."

Maybe Christopher was right about him. Maybe a hundred women have fallen in love with Sutton. I'm just one in a long line. Does that make it any less real? "Well, Freida makes a mean chicken salad. In the fridge, if you're hungry."

One thing about beautiful old houses is that they don't always have modern amenities. There's only enough hot water in the tank for a lukewarm shower, but I turn the knob all the way and stand under the spray without moving, letting it use up all the hot water in a matter of seconds. It burns my shoulders, my breasts. My skin turns pink, which is a relief. That's how I feel on the inside. Tender and hurt. The water turns cold, but I stay like that, opening my mouth and drinking some of the well water, letting it numb me from the outside.

When I get out of the shower, I still look like I've been run over by a train, my eyes red and a little shell-shocked. But I don't look like I've just been in a gangbang, which is an improvement. I throw on a Smith College sweatshirt and a loose pair of sweats.

Then I step into the closet to take deep

breaths.

Five seems like enough, but it's not until ten that I think I'm capable of hiding my grief and shock at how skinny Mom looks these days, at how weak she seems.

I half expect Sutton to be gone. Didn't he disappear when I needed him most? But I can hear his voice as I come down the stairs, low and teasing. And then my mother's voice, answering back.

It feels surreal to walk into the kitchen and see them sitting at the table. Like maybe I fell asleep in the shower and hit my head. This is all a dream, seeing my mother laugh with Sutton.

"What are you doing?" I ask, which is silly considering what they're holding.

"Gin," Sutton says, tipping his cards toward me. "And your mother is kicking my behind."

"And we're having ice cream." My mom tucks the spoon almost delicately into the carton and takes a bite. "If you ask very nice, we'll let you have some."

It takes me a moment to remind my feet to move, but I manage to cross the parquet floor to the kitchen table and take an empty seat. A glance at the cards laid out reveals that, yes, my mother is kicking Sutton's behind. Who uses that word anymore? *Behind.* It's an old-world kind of manners for him to watch his language around my mother.

"I hope you didn't bet anything on the game," I say, picking up a spare spoon.

Sutton nods toward the counter, where a glass case reveals baked goods. "That chocolate chip cookie."

I stare at him, expecting him to suddenly fly around or transform into a dragon. That's how strange it is that he got my mother to eat anything, even ice cream. How strange it is that he got her to want food at all. She's had her share of wheatgrass and barley in her life, and it hasn't helped her that much. Now I'm just thrilled to see her eating anything, to see her cheeks pink with excitement.

She puts down three aces with a little laugh. "That cookie is as good as mine."

I scoot my chair a little closer to Sutton. "You obviously need all the help you can get," I tell him by way of explanation. He gives me a small smile, looking almost bemused.

He's warm against my side, solid, comforting. He drops his hand to clasp mine, two of his fingers filling my palm. And I feel closer to him in this moment than I did at the Den, when he was inside me.

When my mother wins, she gets up to do a funny little jig and get the chocolate chip cookie. Which then prompts her to get milk and cookies out for everyone.

"What are you doing here?" I ask, soft so that only he can hear. I don't only mean in this kitchen. I mean in my life. In my heart. What is he doing to me?

"Not courting you," he murmurs.

That makes me laugh because he's telling the truth. This is Sutton being an ordinary person, kind and genuine and so damn charming he has my mother eating cookies. If he courted me again, I don't think I'd even survive it. He's dangerous, this man. More dangerous than Christopher's cruel indifference.

"The library," I murmur. "It's going to make it, right?"

He raises an eyebrow. "Why do you ask?"

"Because I talked to the foreman yesterday, and he said that they haven't even applied for permits yet. Or ordered supplies. Or started—"

"They have to ascertain the condition of the building first. Better to be thorough now than have surprises later. But you shouldn't be in the library, Harper. Not while the foundation is broken. While the foundation is shaky. It's not safe for you to be there. Promise me."

Safe? I'm not worried about safe. Sometimes having the roof crash down on my head actually seems appealing. A lot more appealing than a neat little Death Plan, that's for sure.

My throat feels tight, and I have to turn away. "Harper?" he says.

I can hear the concern in his voice. He's going to make this about me in a second, but I won't let him. "No," I tell him, as normal as I can. "Keep playing. Please."

Then my mom sits down for another round, and I can turn away blindly, eyes hot with tears, lips pressed tight. I hold it together long enough to make it to my bedroom. I grab a pillow from the bed on my way to the closet before shutting myself inside. And there, with my face pressed into the cotton, muffled to the world around me, I crack into a thousand pieces.

CHAPTER THIRTEEN

DEATH WISH

THE LIBRARY LOOKS like a war zone with temporary plaster columns holding up the ceiling and holes drilled into the precious mosaic floor.

I guess you really do have to break something before you can fix it.

Sutton doesn't want me here, which is why I come after hours. I can think without the jackhammers and sweaty muscled men distracting me. There's something about this broken wall that makes me ache inside, as if a living being has been injured, as if I need to sew it back together so that it can heal. But not with the butt of a buffalo or the heel of a boot.

That might be a more authentic restoration, but it's boring. And I have the sense that it would bury the wall instead of making it come alive.

This library isn't going to be a museum. It will have modern books and computers for the community.

The wall should breathe with the community.

I'm doing my part by smoking a joint while I work, folding the sweet, earthy smell into the clay. I'm not sure it helps me create better, but it definitely makes me more willing to try. Which is how I end up on top of a twenty-foot ladder, holding up a piece of sculpted clay to see how it looks. The ladder wobbles for one second, and I hold my breath.

"Do you have a death wish?"

I know who it is before I look down. The electricity along my skin tells me it's Christopher before I even see his stupid beautiful suit or his dark eyes. Not to mention it's the same thing he said to me years ago when I sat on the railing of the yacht—only a few minutes before I fell into the water. "What are you doing here?"

"Keeping you from breaking your neck."

Why does he care? "In case you haven't noticed, I'm not falling."

"There's always a second time," he says, the grimness of his voice proving he remembers the yacht as clearly as I do. How he'd jumped in to save me. How it remained our secret to this day.

It's a kind of thread, that secret, binding us together no matter how far away he seems.

I climb down the ladder with exaggerated care, making sure I don't even wobble, because he will use any weakness against me. And also because the world is a little spinny right now. Maybe I shouldn't mix pot and ladders. "I'm not speaking to you."

He might as well be the galaxy itself, unfathomable and dark. Nothing I say is going to affect him. At least that's how it seems on the outside. "And you're high. Christ."

"This is my library now. You're not welcome here." I'm ready to tear him apart, to fight off all the arguments he's sure to make. I'm ready to hate him, until his next words.

"What I said about your mother is unforgivable. I have no excuse for it. But I am sorry."

All my anger collapses in on itself, a black hole. God. If he had come here self-righteous and cruel, I could have battled him until the end of time. Which just makes him a bigger asshole. "It doesn't matter," I tell him, which is a lie.

"It matters to me. And if you want to request that someone else manage your trust fund—"

"You'd like that, wouldn't you? Never having to deal with me again."

"I never wanted to have that control. I never asked for it. Sometimes I think your father did it because he knew it would make you hate me. It was the final *fuck you*."

My eyebrows shoot up. "I thought you looked up to my dad."

"I can respect the man and still acknowledge he was a monumental bastard."

"I'm familiar with the feeling," I say drily.

"And then other times I think, maybe it wasn't a *fuck you*. Maybe he was just that dysfunctional that he thought he was protecting you. It could have been his last gesture of care as your father."

My throat burns. "I really think it was the first one."

"You're probably right." He puts his hands into the pockets of his slacks, which somehow doesn't make him look dejected. Instead he looks thoughtful. "Anyway, I don't think it's for the best. Your mom dying."

I swallow around a knot. "No. It's not."

He looks toward the front of the library where a temporary wall has been erected, more protective than the heavy layers of plastic sheeting that were there before. "I have a hard time with…"

"Being nice?"

"I was going to say death. Accepting it."

"A hard time." My laugh sounds hollow. "Yes, I think I have that, too. I don't accept it. I can't. How can anyone accept it? The end of someone you love. It's not a thing you can accept."

He stares at me, his dark eyes opaque, because it doesn't matter what I say. Death doesn't care whether I accept it or not. "Is there anything I can do to help?"

"No." I think of Sutton playing gin with my mother. I can't imagine Christopher doing the same thing, but I'm tired of pushing people away. And that isn't what I need from him anyway. I need something more personal. More selfish. "Maybe."

Christopher leans over the counter and picks up a yellow construction hat. "You should be wearing one of these. This is an active construction zone."

I groan. "Not you, too. Sutton's always on my case."

"It's important, Harper." He places it lightly on my head, and I stick out my tongue.

"How am I supposed to be creative with this thing on? It's like a jail for my head."

"It will keep your head in one piece." He looks up at the wall, studying it. "Did you know they invented the hard hat around the time this was carved? Out in the Hoover Dam, you had these guys on planks of wood hanging on rope seven hundred feet off the ground."

I shiver, looking up. The wall is only thirty feet high.

"They got tired of debris falling and hitting them in the head. Sometimes killing them. So they invented a way to steam canvas, to make it hard enough to protect them."

"You know what's wild? How fragile human beings are, that we actually survived this long."

"My dad had it. Prostate cancer."

A fist around my heart. A squeeze. "I didn't know that."

Or maybe I didn't want to know that about him. Maybe I kept myself closed off to him, the way he kept himself closed off from me the night after the poker game. We're both products of our childhoods, raised not to trust love, determined to buy it so we can see the price up front.

He leans against the library circular, crossing one foot over the other. "He fought it, you know. Doing everything the doctors told him. It was brutal. It killed him faster than the cancer would have."

"I'm sorry," I whisper, and I am. I'm desperately sorry. No one should have to watch their parent die like this. I don't know what kind of death would be better, though. I don't *understand* death, so maybe I'm more naive than I realized.

Or maybe death isn't meant to be understood.

"I don't know… maybe I thought I could spare you that, cutting off the trust fund so it couldn't pay for that experimental treatment. I was relieved when I heard she was going to stop treatment altogether."

My eyes close, pressing out a few tears. They're ever present with me now. I only have to look at something she would have liked in a store, see a food she would have loved to eat before they start falling. I'm a wreck, and she's more at peace than I've ever seen her.

Christopher shakes his head slowly. "Then I saw you that night. You were so lost. I would have done anything to fix that. Found a doctor from across the world. Invented a cure myself."

I reach over the counter and touch the back of his hand. He clasps my hand, even covered with clay and dust. "Who was there for you?" I ask him. "When your father died?"

He blinks, looking uncertain. It's a strange expression on him. Foreign. "What do you mean?"

"Who held your hand? Who let you cry?"

A long silence. "My mother... she was already distant by the time it happened. I think it was almost a relief for her. A way to leave without the shame of getting a divorce."

I make a small sound, unable to help myself. Sympathy.

"It's a blur to me now. And after... after, I just focused on school. That was his thing. Focus on school and get a nice safe nine-to-five job with a retirement plan."

"He'd be proud of you," I whisper.

Christopher looks at me sideways, his expression severe. "I'm not sure about that. I'm the asshole boss of the guys he wanted me to be, but it doesn't matter."

"Of course it matters."

"Death isn't a place in the clouds where people smile down on us. It's pointless, Harper. You want to know why I work so hard to make money? Because it's the only damn thing that's real in this life. Something to hold on to because there damn sure isn't anything at the end."

CHAPTER FOURTEEN

THE COMMON MAN

THE NEXT NIGHT when I arrive at the library there's a very tall, very sturdy metal scaffold waiting for me beside the wall. It could have been anyone who left it here. Maybe the construction foreman wanted to check something at the top of the wall. Or maybe Sutton left it for me to use. But I have a suspicion that it's Christopher.

Does that mean he's going to visit again tonight?

There's a joint in my pocket, but I don't bother to light up. I'm already buzzed, my head floating, my body hot. Christopher Bardot is a potent drug for me; I can only handle him in small doses. Anticipation slides through my veins, and I feel high before he even comes.

Something keeps me from climbing the scaffolding or getting a ladder from the equipment out back. Instead I work with the putty on the ground, keeping one eye trained on the door in case I have another late-night visitor.

It gets to be so late that I doubt he's coming, and then I have to face the hard lump of disappointment in my gut, the proof that I want the man I shouldn't.

As if the cute little dress I'm wearing tonight didn't already prove that.

It's with those disheartened eyes that I look at the putty I've been working with, surprised to find it's actually pretty good. It's a more abstract piece than I usually make—geometric shapes unfolding, like an idea being peeled away. Or maybe skin flayed open, in a purely conceptual way. That would be an interesting addition to the wall, exposing what's underneath. Not in a literal sense, because there's only shadow and studs back there, but symbolically.

What *is* behind the wall? I'm not sure I know the answer. Industry is on the surface. Muscles and iron and longing. What's underneath must be darker. It always is. The opposite of industriousness… well, that's being stationary. Being stuck. Maybe even failure.

The opposite of longing is despair, the certainty that what you want will never come.

"It's not your usual style," comes a low voice from behind me.

Christopher steps through the archway, wearing black slacks and leather loafers, a stark contrast to the dusty disarray of the library. He's unbuttoned the top of his white dress shirt, but it still looks crisp. His jacket straight. Every black hair on his head neatly in place.

He looks around with a hard expression, as if the building's being inspected by him and failing to impress. As if he still owns the place. That makes me frown. "How did you get in through there? The doors back there are locked."

"It's possible I didn't send all the keys to the commercial realtor," he says, not sounding very remorseful. He also doesn't offer to give me the secret key, and for some reason I don't demand it. The library is about open knowledge, not locked doors, and Lord knows Christopher isn't going to vandalize anything. I'm more likely to do that than anyone else.

But I think the real reason is that I want him to come back.

"Why are you here?" I ask softly.

"To make sure you don't fall and break your neck. It's a habit of yours."

"Only when you're around. And I don't mean

the library. Why are you *here*, in Tanglewood, developing the land I didn't buy from you? You could have sold it."

He shrugs. "You know me. For money. For stepping on the backs of the common man."

For the first time since I met him, his words ring false, as if he spoke a lie. As if everything else he said to me has been true. "Be careful," I whisper. "I might think you want to stay near me."

He takes a step closer, and I'm suddenly aware that my hands are caked with putty. The world of art shows is glamorous with wine and chandeliers, but the reality of creation is much more messy.

And a little more dangerous.

At one point I was so engrossed in my work, so vehement with a sculpting tool that the metal detached from the wood handle and plunged into my thumb. It bled into my dress for a while, and every time I worked the clay after that, smoothed it over and made it ridge, the newly formed scab would break again. There are dark striations in the finished product—not red blood now, but an ominous black.

Christopher takes my hand and turns it over, pulling away the clay where it's formed a protective barrier. He makes a *tsk* sound, probably because I'm careless. Because I have a death wish. Because I don't wear a suit and move numbers around on paper all day. It makes me want to smack him, that sound; why can't I be good enough for him? *He isn't your father,* Avery said, but this sinking feeling in my stomach is exactly the same.

Except Christopher does something I don't expect, something I never would have imagined. He presses his open mouth against my thumb, his lips unexpectedly gentle, his tongue sweeping over the cut. There's clay and blood and sweat, right there against his tongue. He must taste every dream I have, every failure I fear. He must taste *me.*

His eyes close, lashes long and black against his cheek, and he moans. He moans as if I'm some sweet nectar he never imagined tasting. I've had this man's cock in my mouth, and still this is the most unabashedly sensual experience of my life. He sucks gently, the suction of his mouth on my thumb somehow reaching straight to my clit, pulling me taut, making my legs press together.

When he looks up at me again, his eyes are hooded. "You know I want you. You've always known I wanted you, and you got into so much trouble because you loved when I came after you."

My laugh feels a little shaky, like I'm walking a tightrope high above the ground, praying that I'll keep my balance long enough to reach the other side. "I don't get into trouble. Trouble gets into me. That would happen whether you were there to save me or not."

His lips quirk up. "But you do love it when I come after you."

"Is that why you're here? Am I in trouble?"

"No," he murmurs against my palm, pressing a burning kiss against my lifeline. "I thought we would try something new this time. I'm not here to save you or protect you. I'm not here to catch you when you fall. So I'd recommend not climbing anything."

That makes me laugh, though it's more an exhalation of disbelief. He has always been the white knight to my damsel in distress. It's been a gift as much as a curse, a way to keep himself near me without ever being vulnerable. "What would you even do with me if you weren't catching me?"

"I have some ideas," he says in a voice like black gravel, rough and sliding. He steps close enough that I can feel his body heat against me, that I can smell the musk of a day's work in the office, the grit and determination of him made real.

My voice comes out a whisper. "I don't know what to do with myself if I'm not falling."

Two fingers under my chin. He gazes down at me with fierce possession. "Catch me instead."

There are only two seconds in which I might reclaim my sanity. Two seconds when I might remember that he's dynamite and I'm flame. I use them to lean closer, savoring the brush of his breath against my lips. Every nerve ending in my body lights up in anticipation. His hand slides to the back of my neck, and I surrender to the certain explosion, letting my head fall back, my eyes close. His teeth sink into my bottom lip. Starbursts flare behind my eyelids.

I've been with Christopher a million times in my imagination. If I had a dollar for every time he pressed his lean body over mine... I'd be rich with it, swimming in money.

The times with Sutton should have been the real thing.

They should have been reality, but this, *this* feels brand-new.

He doesn't kiss me; that would be too easy for a man like this. He's made of sharp edges, and he uses them to leave a mark. He bites at my mouth like someone long starved, made violent with it. Strong fingers grasp my hair. The groan he makes sinks into me—a barbed-wire sound. I'm pinned from all sides by him, panting in his hold, whimpering so he knows I don't want him to let go.

It only seems to inflame him; he walks forward, forcing me back against the scaffolding, cold metal bars crossing my back. It's too much, too much, and I take a swipe at his lips with my teeth.

Only then does he gentle. It's like he was waiting for me to fight back, like that's what he needed all along. Maybe that's what he meant when he said *save me*; maybe I have to hurt him to do it.

I pull at his white dress shirt, his jacket, but he's made too solid to move. The only way to reach him is through my mouth, and I nip at him wherever I can reach—his lips, his chin, the angle of his jaw. He sucks in a breath, but it doesn't sound like pain. It sounds like someone who's felt something too good, and he backs up that impression by pushing his hips against me. There's an outline there, unmistakable. Hot and hard against my belly. Sutton is large, but Christopher is made of steel—not just in his cock, but his abs, his arms. Everywhere I can reach, he's forged with fire.

Except for his throat. There the skin is tender, almost velvet, with a late-night bristle that burns my cheek. I slip my tongue out to taste him; he's elemental earth. He vibrates at the slickness, tilting his head back so I can reach better. I move down, down, down in defiance, pressing my lips to the hollow at the base, feeling his heartbeat move through him.

"Please," he says, and he sounds so lost. He sounds like I feel most of the time. I never imagined that Christopher Bardot would bare the most vulnerable part of his body.

Never imagined that he would beg.

This is someone always in command, the smartest man in the room, the most determined. And when he cedes control to me, power rushes through my veins. I can do anything if this man needs me.

Anything except decide what to do next. Despite the wildness of our threesome in the Den, despite Sutton's creativity, I'm not really that experienced when it comes to sex. I don't really know what *normal* sex looks like, and I'm pretty sure that's not what Christopher would want anyway.

He solves the problem by pulling away long enough to yank off his jacket. He lays it down over the dusty floor, ruining the expensive fabric. "For your knees," he says, and I remember the salt-sweet taste of his cock in my mouth. I drop down, too eager, but then he's beside me. Under me.

And I realize that none of Sutton's creativity prepared me for this—for Christopher lying flat on the bits of rubble, only half-shielded by his jacket. For my knees on either side of his head, padded by his jacket, the pale peach cotton of my dress spread out over him. It's only shock that has me reeling back, only shock that has me gasping, "No. Wait. Don't."

Even so I'm not expecting him to actually stop, to push my skirt away long enough to ask in hard, explicit terms, "You don't want me to lick your cunt?"

My hips react in a visceral way to the word *cunt*; they rock forward as if asking for his tongue, needing it. Sutton pressed me up against a wall and held me there. Christopher ordered me onto Sutton's cock and fucked my mouth. There's a certain amount of helplessness I can pretend in those situations—I didn't know his mouth would make me orgasm. I couldn't predict his lap would have a stiff cock pointing up.

And even if those kinds of nonexcuses only

work in my head, I didn't realize how much I was relying on them before now. Before now when I have to place my body over Christopher's face and lower my sex to his mouth. There's too much action involved, too much knowledge.

I can't, I can't, at least until he says, "I've been dreaming about this. Since that night I held you naked in the cabin. I knew I shouldn't think about you that way. I had just pulled you out of the goddamn water, but it was all I wanted. I dreamed about you waking up and kneeling down on top of me. I dreamed about how you would taste—salty from the bay, sweet from your sex. I'd lick you and lick you until you were dripping down my face, until I was slippery with you, and then you'd come, riding me hard enough I'd barely be able to breathe, and I'd reach down and grip my cock. That's all it would take. I'd just hold myself and come while you moaned my name above me."

"I want that too," I breathe. None of my imaginary sex dreams prepared me for this, but every nerve ending has come awake. There's an ache between my legs, and I'm afraid he's ruined me. Something in me cracked when I heard him speak just now, and the only way I'll ever be assuaged will be with a mouth under my spread legs while I rock my hips just how I want it.

Only, I would have thought I'd have more power on top like this. His hands grasp my ass, somehow covering almost all of it, even though there should really be too much. He holds enough to mold my movements, to rock me to his beat instead of mine. It's too fast at first, and I gasp above him. I don't even have any balance, and I'm forced to hold on to the bars of the scaffolding that shoots up around us. The old rusty wheels complain at the pressure, but they hold still, locked into place.

He licks me through the cotton, but it does nothing to disguise the feel of him. It only seems to make it sharper, the wet fabric pressing into my folds, into my clit. All I can do is hold on as he searches for something that makes me squirm.

And then he bites me, teeth only slightly blunted through the cotton, right on my clit, and I scream a little, making birds fly up from somewhere in the library where they shouldn't be. His hands pull me toward him again and again, there's no escaping the sun-blinding pleasure, and then I'm coming, a mess of slick arousal sounding slippery against his lips.

Christopher doesn't reach down to grasp his cock, even though I moan his name. Instead he flips me over so I'm on the ground looking up at the crack in the wall. A zipper. A tear. And then he's above me, inside me, my legs spread so wide I'm almost bent in half. His face looks carved into sharp angles, his eyes hard black stone. Everything about this is too much. "I should be high for this," I gasp, and I expect him to tell me that I shouldn't be, not ever, it isn't safe, isn't legal.

"Later," is all he manages to say, and it rings through my body like a bell. Keeping time, that bell. A promise that I'll hear it again, and I arch my body up in gratitude.

His cock pushes deeper, and I have to squirm away from the fullness.

He seems to think I'm hurting, because he murmurs, "I'm sorry." One hand curves beneath my neck, the other beneath the small of my back. He's holding me up away from the ground even as he fucks me into it, shielding me even as he tears me apart.

I'm not expecting to come again, but then he shifts his hips. He hits some new angle, and my hands fly up above my head. It's like I'm falling, even though I'm already at the bottom. My hand finds one pole of the scaffold, and I hold on tight. Pleasure rises inside me, sharp and sudden. Christopher quickens in three hard thrusts, and then he's holding me so tight I can't breathe, my climax taking me just as swiftly. I'm held suspended in the air by his embrace, floating beneath the shaky scaffold and the broken wall. It's as if the whole building shudders when we come. There's dust in my eyes. Dust, dust. That's why they burn.

I'M NOT SURE what I expected after sex beneath the scaffolding. Maybe that Christopher would disappear into the shadows, making me wonder if it was just a dream. Or maybe he'd say something mean about how rich girls don't have feelings and I'd have to awkwardly flounce out of the building that I own, like that disaster of a dinner at Koi.

Instead he puts my clothing back to rights with careful determination. His expression remains grave even as his fingers brush my bare skin. Then he stands.

His shirt looks a little rumpled, his hair askew, but otherwise he doesn't look like he just had sex. And he definitely doesn't look like someone just came while sitting on his face.

"Come on," he says, holding out his hand.

I narrow my eyes, untrusting. "Where are we going?"

"To my lair," he says, his voice sardonic. "Where I'm going to have my way with you."

When Christopher Bardot argues with me he's attractive, but when he does this dry humor he's downright irresistible. Somehow my cheeks are warm. "Haven't you already done that?"

A dark gaze runs over my dress, leaving goose bumps in its wake. A heartbeat remains between my legs, an insistent throb where his cock has been. "Not nearly enough."

"Lead the way," I manage to say lightly, as if this is all a big joke. I have a lot of practice with that—pretending that life is a joke instead of tragic. "I've always wanted to see your lair."

A light mist kisses my face when we step outside. My dress doesn't warm me nearly as well as the jeans and T-shirt I usually wear. Cool night air slides up my legs, and I shiver in the black parking lot.

"Cold?" he asks, but he doesn't wait for an answer. The jacket that had been slung over his arm drapes over my shoulders suffusing me with the scent of earth and sex and something purely Christopher. It should probably repel me, but I find myself drawing the material tighter around me.

He takes my hand again as we cross the parking lot, and even in the black of night I can't help feeling safe. It reminds me of sinking, sinking into the ocean. And Christopher diving in to save me. It created an unbreakable line between whatever neuron in my brain between him and safety. When I'm scared I think of him—and how he would protect me. When I'm happy I wish he were with me to experience it, too. If it were anyone else I would have called this feeling love, but I don't understand how my heart can betray me with someone who so clearly doesn't love me back.

We cross the slippery gravel of the library's parking lot and a cracked street. Then we're standing in front of a half-built building that looks like it was transplanted out of upscale downtown. Frosted windows do nothing to obscure the marble floors inside or the wide bank of elevators.

"Is this what your half of the library built?" I ask, to remind myself that he only wants to use me. For money. For sex. Sometimes those are the same things, anyways.

It doesn't mean he has feelings for me.

"Construction has been underway since you

left," he says, in a matter-of-fact voice. "My share of the money is sitting in a bank account. What do you think I should spend it on?"

I think of the way the scaffolding seemed to tremble with the aftershocks of our orgasms. The way the building seems to breathe harder every day, struggling to stay upright. All that money to house books, because knowledge is the only thing that has a chance in hell of saving the west side. I look around at the dilapidated buildings on either side, the way they seem to slouch beside the monument to commercial success between them. "Books," I say simply.

He gives me an enigmatic smile. "Maybe then I'll finally learn."

Sliding glass doors silently open as we approach. I raise my eyebrow. "You have it open."

A nod toward a black sphere jutting from the metal frame. "Facial recognition."

"That's not a little big brother-ish?"

"Big brother is the government. This is a privately owned building, which means we can be as intrusive as we want. Do you have something to hide?"

"Everything," I say. "Most of it from myself."

He presses the button for an elevator, and the doors slide open. "After you," he says, a wave of his arm gesturing me inside. It feels a little like a spider speaking to the fly, but I step inside the elevator and we're both whisked higher and higher, the lighted buttons rising.

The doors open directly onto the roof, the concrete almost unearthly pristine white. Not enough rain or dirt or time has stained this place, its white floor and short walls and exposed silver pipes. This high it feels like the stars are dangling in front of me, like I can reach out and touch them with my forefinger.

"Oh my God," I say, taking in the view of the city. "It's lovely." Downtown might as well be the next galaxy. And around us there are a hundred thousand pieces of debris orbiting the building. It seems impossible that we can ever get enough inertia to even leave, much less turn this place into a bustling center of commerce. It's both beautiful and heartbreaking, a combination I'm all too familiar with.

"Yes," he says, sounding distracted. "Lovely."

When I glance at him he turns away from me. "Thought you might as well see what you're fighting for."

A lump forms in my throat. "You mean what I'm fighting against."

I know that libraries help communities. That

art can save lives. I believe in the power of them both, but looking at the wasteland that is the west side of Tanglewood it's hard to believe that anything can help.

"Why did you decide to build here?"

"You know why. Cheap real estate. A monopoly on the market."

Selfish reasons, but they don't quite ring true. Not anymore. "Is that all?"

He points toward the library. From this angle the broken stained glass dome at the top looks like a gaping hole where the heart used to be. "You can see the cracks in the foundation from here. Look at the height of this side of the building. And then the other side."

My heart thumps a scared little sound. "Only a little bit."

"I've looked out the windows here for six months. I've seen the whole building shudder and shiver and end up one centimeter more uneven."

"That's why I have a construction crew. They're going to fix it."

"They're not," he says, sounding almost sad. "Nothing can fix the building."

"But Sutton said—"

"Sutton Mayfair would risk your goddamn neck just to get back at me. Don't believe a damn word he says to you. You need to be in a hard hat before you're anywhere near that building. And I don't see why you should be near it at all."

"You don't own the library anymore, and you never owned me. With that attitude no wonder you aren't with someone. Women don't like being ordered around."

"You seemed to like it at the poker game," he says, his voice low.

A flush climbs my cheeks. At the poker game I felt used in a decadent, purely sexual way—but the sex we had under the scaffold was different. It felt like I was the one using Christopher's body, controlling him, *breaking* him like a beautiful stallion.

God, no wonder Sutton wanted Christopher. He knew what it could be like.

"Maybe I like ordering you around." My voice comes out low and liquid, a form of seduction I didn't know I was capable of until I see Christopher's eyes darken. "Does a powerful woman turn you on?"

He studies me with those inky black eyes. "Yes," he says, but though that word reveals so much, it still feels like he's holding even more inside. Like I'd have to pry him open to find out all his secrets. I'm a little afraid of what I'd find if

I did.

"Do you think it would have been different?" I ask, a little wistful. "That kiss in the art gallery. Do you think we would have really dated if my father hadn't written you into the will?"

He stares at me, his eyes stormy, no sense of stillness now. "Dated? You think I would have dated you and then… what? We would have had an argument about working long hours or being jealous or whatever the fuck normal people fight about?"

"I don't know," I whisper, a strange sense of longing tightening my throat.

It would have been nice to find out.

"We wouldn't have dated," he informs me, his voice rim. "I would have claimed you. And what's more you would have claimed me. There wouldn't have been an end. You want to know if it would be different? Day and night, that's how different it would be."

This way is night, dark and a little scary. He doesn't have to spell that part out for me to recognize that truth. "Why did we let Daddy mess it up?"

"We were young. And I was stupid."

"You aren't young anymore." And he's a long way from stupid.

He gives me a private smile, as if he knows a secret. "No, not anymore."

It sounds like a promise, those words. As if he's going to fix what's been broken for so long, but some things are damaged right down to their core. Some things can't ever be put back together. The library looks up at us, its windows shattered and boarded, its walls caving in.

CHAPTER FIFTEEN

THE DANGERS OF CORPORATE EXCESS

I BURN MY hand pulling a tray out of the oven. Metal heated to four hundred degrees burned right through the cute dish towel I found at a boutique that says, *My safeword is takeout.*

"Shit!" I suck on my thumb with a plaintive sound.

Avery gives me a completely unsympathetic snort. "I'll do it."

She uses an oven mitt—a plain, utilitarian blue oven mitt that seems to protect her just fine, because she manages to put the tray on the stove without almost dropping it.

"I bow to your greatness, Martha Stewart," I say, handing her a serving spoon.

We spent the afternoon carving pumpkins. Avery made a traditional jack-o-lantern face. I applied my Smith College art school education to sculpting a penis out of a large orange fruit. And then we cleaned off the seeds, added plenty of butter and salt, and roasted them to perfection. My mouth is watering just looking at them, all browned and glistening.

When we've got the pumpkin seeds in a bowl, we join my mother on the sofa, where she's got the TV queued up to the title screen of *An Affair to Remember.* "Ready, girls?"

"I've never seen this one," Avery says.

"That's blasphemy," my mother says. "This is the most romantic movie."

I go for a cluster of pumpkin seeds and pop it into my mouth. It burns my tongue. Then the salt and flavor hit me all at once. *Orgasmic.* "I've seen this a million times. And sometimes she'll replay the scene at the end, the one where he sees her in the theater."

Mom's eyes get all dreamy. "And then he goes to her apartment."

"'I was looking up,'" I say in my best Deborah Kerr impression. Avery gives me a bemused smile. "You'll understand in about two hours. And you'll never look at the Empire State Building the same way. In fact it's almost like the movie is a statement on the dangers of corporate excess."

"Oh hush," Mom says, pressing play. "It's pure romance."

The three of us gorge ourselves on butter-coated pumpkin seeds, licking our fingers to get all the salt. Cary Grant and Deborah fall in love on their cruise, even though they're engaged to other people. *Pure romance,* my mother said. And it's true. This is one of the most romantic movies ever made, except for the woman Cary Grant's character didn't marry. The man Deborah's character didn't marry. Strange, how love makes everything understandable. Even if it breaks someone else's heart.

We reach the middle of the movie when I realize my mother's fallen asleep, her head tilted to the side, the blueish veins visible in her eyelids. A knot in my throat, I pull up a blanket around her waist.

"Should I stop the movie?" Avery whispers.

I shake my head, but it's not really an answer. Part of me wants to shake her, to demand she stay awake long enough to watch her favorite few minutes of her favorite movie. She's been sleeping more and more, sleeping in late, taking naps.

The nurse told me it would happen.

Frieda also told me to consider a hospice facility, because this is one of many signs that my mother is dying. Her lack of appetite. The bruises that appear on her body even when she didn't fall down. The way she sometimes wakes up without knowing where she is.

A hospice isn't going to make that better. No, I should be the one who reminds her gently where she is. I should be the one who coaxes my mother to eat, who sits in vigil beside her while she sleeps.

I take her hand in mine, feeling how terribly cold it is. Unnaturally cold. That's another sign from the nurse. Fevers and drops in temperature that come and go. *How long?* I asked her, but the nurse, so full of information, hadn't wanted to answer that. It could be anywhere from a week to six months. *Then you don't really know.* That's what I wanted to scream at her. Instead I just thanked her with tears in my eyes, stupid, useless tears.

Avery hits the pause button on the remote and comes to kneel in front of us. "I'm sorry," she whispers. "Is there anything I can do?"

"She'll probably sleep for a couple hours," I say, shaking my head.

A small smile. "I mean for you."

That makes me laugh, a watery, strangled sound. "I don't know."

Avery takes my other hand, holding it as gently as I'm holding my mother's hand. We remain linked like that, a chain of solidarity against an enemy that none of us can fight. And maybe that is what I need. Someone to sit here, quiet and still, not asking for anything.

Dark falls around the house, taking away the purple glow. "You should get home," I murmur, my voice rusty as if I've been crying, but I haven't been, not tonight. It's like my body feels it the same way, even the times when I can hold in the tears.

"I can stay in a guest room," Avery says, her hazel eyes troubled.

"Is Gabriel home?" I'm asking about more than his travel arrangements. I'm asking about whether he still feels distant to her. If she needs a place to stay as much as I need her to be here.

She bites her lip. "He had to extend his China trip."

"Oh. Then by all means, stay in the guest room. We can watch the grand finale tomorrow morning over French toast, which is maybe the only thing that tastes better than roasted pumpkin seeds."

"Do you think…"

I squeeze her hand gently. "Do I think what?"

"Do you think he would do that?" A glance

toward the black TV screen. "You know, find someone else while he's traveling. Fall in love with her while I'm so far away."

"Oh God. Oh, honey, no. I shouldn't have let you see that movie."

"No, of course you should. It's her favorite movie." She glances at my mother's face, her expression softening. "She deserves to watch whatever she wants to watch."

"Gabriel Miller would never cheat on you."

"Right," she says, but she doesn't sound sure.

"And if he did, I would cut off his balls and feed them to—"

"He probably isn't cheating. I just wish he'd come home."

The hint of doubt in her eyes makes me furious. Not the kind of furious where I want to yell at someone or stomp around. The kind of furious that's cold and empty. Helpless. That's what it makes me feel. Which is exactly what my mother's cancer makes me feel.

CHAPTER SIXTEEN

THE SUIT

HELPLESS.

The word stays with me through the rest of the long night, through dreams of kings and goblins. I wake restless, as if something has been uncovered—but I don't know what. I spend the day giving my mother a manicure, a mud mask. A whole spa day in the comfort of her own bathroom. Only after dinner, when I put her to bed, when she drifts to sleep, do I get in my leased BMW and drive to the library.

My tools are neatly stashed in the trunk. The place that I park is right next to the side door, which has a lock. I normally step inside and get to work, my mind already spinning with ideas of new things to try with the wall. Except tonight I'm more interested in what's outside the library.

It's not only being in this building, Harper. It's

*the whole damn west side. We want to revitalize it,
but it hasn't happened yet. That means it's full of
crime and violence. It's fucking dangerous.*

There are cracks in the sidewalk, pieces of the
curb missing. Large potholes in the street. Those
things didn't really stand out against the backdrop
of a building blasted to pieces, but of course this
damage must have been here before Christopher
and Sutton ever purchased the land.

Behind the library there's an uneven parking
lot that ends with a chain-link fence around the
construction happening on the Bardot Tower.
They aren't stuck in an infinite cycle of evaluation
like the library, because they tore down whatever
poor building stood there. I hate Christopher for
his efficient dismantling of the past. And I envy
him, too.

Low animal sounds slow my step. It sounds
almost like the growl of a rabid dog in the
alleyway up ahead. The hair on the back of my
neck rises. I should turn around and go inside the
library. No, if I were really concerned with safety,
I'd get back in my car and drive home. *Do you
have a death wish?* Christopher asked me the
question the first day we met, when he found me
on the railing of the yacht smoking a joint. Maybe
I do have a death wish, or at least morbid

curiosity, because I keep creeping forward. Brick is cool against my palms as I lean close to peek around the wall.

There isn't a wild animal, at least not in the usual sense. Instead there's a man with his back against the library, his head thrown back, his hands grasping the hair of a girl at his feet.

His rough sounds bounce off the walls on either side, her wet sucking sounds the most sexually graphic thing I've ever heard in my life. I'm standing with my mouth open, more shocked than I would have thought to see sex performed so publicly… so degradingly. I've seen plenty of frat party shenanigans, even a few that went down in the record books. Girls on girls. Multiple partners. Drunken acrobatics.

None of them come close to this.

He turns them so she's against the wall, him shuffling with his jeans around his ankles. Then he thrusts into her hard and fast, so hard her sounds become louder, his ass muscles tensing on every push forward. He looks down at the top of her head like it's the hottest thing he's ever seen. Her hands are splayed against the brick behind her, holding her up in a crouch.

A roar and then he's coming into her mouth, pressing his hips flush against her face. I watch as her hands fist, my insides twisted with worry for her throat, for her ability to breathe. I take a step forward, ready to intervene, when finally he lets her go. She falls to the ground, panting against the gravel and decades' worth of detritus. He zips up, still panting loudly enough to be heard from twenty feet away. Then he pulls something out of his pocket. Money? He tosses it onto the floor in front of her before leaving the alleyway toward the street.

God. *God.* He just paid her for that blowjob. My body is confused as hell, torn between being hot at the explicit sexual display and angered by an act she probably did not enjoy.

Someone from my sorority was a cam girl. One corner of her room was decorated with frilly pink pillows and carefully placed composition notebooks and banners from a nonexistent sorority so she couldn't be traced. Sometimes we would join her for a playful little striptease to watch the horny Internet anons go crazy and make enough money to order shots at the bar later. She didn't enjoy what she did, not in a sexual way. It was a job to her, the way you might be a clerk at the bookstore or a waitress at the diner off campus. She didn't get off on it, but she did like the money. And she had options. It wasn't a last resort to her, but as I watch the girl snatch the money and shove it into her shoe, I think this isn't a choice for her.

She stands gingerly, wiping her mouth with the back of her hand. "You like the show?"

I stand there in silent shock before I'm sure she's talking to me. There's no point in hiding anymore, so I take a step into the alleyway, my body still flushed in confused arousal. "I'm sorry."

"There's usually a charge for someone watching."

"I didn't mean to... but I can pay you." I fumble for my purse, feeling slow and disconnected. This was happening outside the library, maybe every single night that I was inside, sculpting as if I could change the world with *art*. "How much is it? Never mind, I can just give you what I have—"

A harsh laugh. "Don't worry about it. I know you weren't with him."

"How do you know?"

"Besides the fact that you look like you stepped out of an ad for Anthropologie? Because he's a regular. And he doesn't bring girls around or ask for anything more complicated than a BJ."

There are things more complicated than that blowjob? Because it looked intense and difficult, every movement with subtle undertones of power.

"A regular. Do you live around here?"

"Guess you could say that. I stay closer to here than you do, I'm guessing."

"You're making a lot of assumptions based on jeans and a T-shirt."

"Am I wrong?"

That makes me laugh. "Nah, I guess I'm easy to read."

"I'm surprised you stuck around once you saw what was happening. You a perv?"

"I don't know. Maybe. I didn't know that it was a… you know, a professional situation at first."

She giggles, which unsettles me because of how young she sounds. "A professional. Well, I'm not putting on a suit and carrying my briefcase into work, but yeah, I'm a pro."

I take a few steps closer, but the shadows don't reveal her face to me. "How old are you, anyway?"

That makes her stop laughing. "You aren't a cop, are you?"

"God no."

"It's none of your damn business how old I am." The bravado in her voice doesn't scare me. It just makes me sad that she needs such strong defenses. "So go get your pervy kicks somewhere else."

She takes a step back, and panic rises in my throat. "Wait. Let me give you the cash I have with me. It's not that much, but it should be a couple nights at a motel or something."

That makes her pause, at least. "That's what you are. A Mother Theresa."

I'm the one who snorts a laugh. "Definitely not."

"You want to save me? You want to protect me from the big bad wolves of the world?"

"I don't—" Except of course I do. "I just want to help, like a tiny bit. That's all."

There's a pause while she wanders forward, almost as if she *is* a deer walking through the forest, unknowing of the dangers within. Then she's a few feet away. The eyeliner can't hide the hurt in her eyes. Her lips are still swollen and slick from the blowjob. This is why the community needs a library; this is why they need art that looks like hope. Because the west side takes girls and turns them into prostitutes. It leaves them on their hands and knees with money lying on the pavement. Books are the answer to this. Knowledge and a safe space in which to learn it.

"I'm not some kind of fashion genius," she says, her voice hard and cold. "I figured you were the library girl as soon as I saw you."

"The library girl?"

"The one who painted the library and made it fall down."

There's a wealth of condemnation in that voice. I wasn't the reason the wrecking ball went into the front of the library, but I blame myself that I didn't stop it sooner. "I'm sorry."

"Nah, it wasn't so bad. I had a stash of the painted pieces for a while. That shit was like gold. I'd sell them for twenty bucks when people would come around during the day."

Twenty bucks, and those people would turn around and sell them online for hundreds, maybe thousands of dollars. My stomach twists with a sense of hopelessness. "I'm so sorry."

"Now you just sound like the suit."

"The what?"

She nods toward the library. Over the roof a skyscraper rises, gleaming in the wasteland. "The suit. He owns that building. Has eyes that look like coffee without any cream or sugar."

Comes around to pay for rough blowjobs from desperate young women? Bile rises in my throat. I never had any right to expect monogamy from Christopher Bardot, but I pictured him with soap opera actresses and local socialites. "Is he…"

I have to swallow down the acid before I can finish. "Is he a customer?" *Don't break my heart, Christopher.*

"Nah," she says, oblivious to the way relief fills me, warmth in my cold limbs. "He never touches me. But he gives me money whenever he comes down. Whatever he has with him, like you're trying to do."

I never would have expected that of Christopher. It makes me feel uneasy in my own skin, as if I'm a little itchy, sitting inside a world that doesn't fit me anymore. "He does?" I ask faintly.

"It's different when he gives me money, though, 'cause if he ever wanted a fuck, I'd give it to him for free anyway. I figure it's kind of like a deposit until he gets hard up."

That makes me laugh. "You wouldn't consider the money I give you an advance?"

"Nah, you aren't gonna fuck me. I already know. Besides that's part of the deal with the suit. He told me to keep an eye on you. If any of my johns give you a hard time, I'm supposed to call him."

CHAPTER SEVENTEEN
TOTALLY MY BUSINESS

I WANT TO seek out Christopher, but something holds me back. It's been bothering me since the night of the poker game, questions half-formed and smoky in my head. Only Sutton can tell me the truth about this.

Except Sutton isn't here.

He works at the library every day with the crew. He's the main person I talk to, how I know about the many, many problems they've found. The foundation problems.

The plumbing leaks. The termites. The broken pipes.

If testosterone were to stand up and walk around, it would look like Asher Cook. The foreman of the construction crew wears a white T-shirt, always crisp and clean in the morning. He's the only person here I actually know, now that

Sutton's disappeared.

Always smudged in dirt and sweat by the end of the day.

His muscles bulge in a way that looks explicit, even fully clothed. A beard does little to hide his constantly surly expression. Dark eyebrows slash over pale green eyes, making me shiver every time he glances at me. He has a yellow hard hat, like everyone else, but frankly his head is probably made of tougher material. As if to prove the point, I find him hanging from the ceiling like some kind of explorer on Mount Kilimanjaro, some kind of complicated tool in his hand, shouting measurements to someone on the ground taking notes. From twenty feet in the air he manages to scowl when he sees me.

Which just makes my smile more cheerful. "Hello, Mr. Cook. Have you seen Sutton?"

At a rough gesture a pulley system lowers him to the ground. "Come with me." He doesn't wait for me to respond. His long strides take him halfway across the library before I catch up to him.

Asher stops at the wall so suddenly I almost fall into him.

I stand there looking for Sutton, because that must be why he brought me here. Except there's no one around. He gestures impatiently toward a tall metal structure on wheels. "Where the hell did this come from?"

"I don't know, it was just there one day." *From Christopher*, my mind helpfully supplies. This seems to confirm that he had it moved here for me. Like he can pull anything out of his pocket, even sea salt grilled edamame and forty foot scaffolding towers.

"Hell," he mutters. "I suppose that's better than you using our ladders."

A huff escapes me. "I put them back where I found them."

His pale green gaze could sear a hole straight through me. "After drawing graffiti all over the expensive fiberglass. In permanent marker. Don't think I didn't see that."

"Knowing my luck they're probably worth a fortune on the Internet." I have a tendency for turning straw into gold, but it doesn't feel like a blessing lately. Is this how Daddy felt? For maybe the first time in my life I feel an similarity with the man who fathered me. Money comes easy, but love is the elusive dream, the one thing always out of reach.

Asher makes a low sound of dissent. "I don't want to sell the ladders on the Internet. I want my men to use them, not jack off to them. And you should be wearing a hard hat inside the building. It's not safe for you to be here without one."

"Is it my fault your men would jack off to hand-drawn images of the goddess Circe? If that had been on a thousand-year-old cave, it would have been a sociological marvel. Because I'm born in the present time it's suddenly 'graffiti.'" I make quotes with my fingers, and I swear, there's a hint of a smile beneath that unruly beard before he frowns.

"This is serious. Hard hat or get the fuck out."

In that case I'll be getting the fuck out. "Have you seen Sutton?"

Asher looks uncomfortable, which makes me wonder if it's more than coincidence. Is Sutton avoiding me? "He isn't coming in today," Asher says finally. "He went to his ranch."

"Right," I say, trying not to sound deflated. "His ranch."

What does it mean?

Probably nothing, I tell myself, but I can't quite believe the lie.

I create new pieces with clay and use the new scaffolding to place them high, examining them in the afternoon light. The clay is only for me to test how things will look, because I go through ten ideas. And then ten more. And then throw it all away to start over.

Usually I'm decisive when it comes to my art. That's why I can paint a wall in one night without stopping. Inspiration drives me until I'm done. With the wall I'm all over the place. I'm not sure what makes this piece so different. Maybe because it's not a blank canvas. It's someone else's art, and I'm trying to add to it. Or maybe the wall is just a metaphor.

It could be there's a crack inside me, too.

Maybe my ability to create art is breaking, breaking, gone.

IN DESPERATION I go to the library during the day, hoping that the sunlight will give me a fresh perspective. Sutton would usually yell at me for being in the library at all, for being here without a hard hat, but he's gone.

My inspiration on the sculptures goes from bad to worse. I can't even bring myself to mix a batch of clay. Instead I order twelve pumpkins from grocery delivery and carve them one after the other, until my hands are a sticky mess. I don't carve cocks… at least, not all the pumpkins are cocks. I've been sculpting things that would fit into the giant crack in the wall—so really, it's no wonder my mind turned dirty.

By the time evening falls on the third day, I've made up my mind, but I still drive home. Mom and I share chicken noodle soup and freshly baked biscuits, which came out pretty amazing considering I got them from the refrigerated aisle. I pulled at the corner of the wrapper until it popped, startling both of us and making us laugh.

Her sleep patterns are all over the place lately. Instead of nodding off early, she stays awake all night, sorting through old photo albums of Dad and her and me when I was a baby. She finally falls asleep by the time the nurse shows up, and even though I haven't slept, I get in my car and head out of the city.

The ranch is an hour away from Tanglewood, but the drive feels quicker now. Sand streams through the funnel faster and faster. I don't bother to knock on the door. I met his sister six months ago. She hated me on sight; she's hardly going to be more welcoming to me now.

Instead I head straight for the stables.

I half expect Sutton to already be working; don't ranchers wake up at three a.m. or something ridiculous? The sun already stretches across the rolling green.

The *empty* rolling green.

Dew gathers on my rose-gold leather flats. I'm wearing skinny jeans and a boatneck T-shirt that says *Namaste in Bed.* My hair is in a messy bun that looks pretty cute considering I tied it back before getting out of the car.

The stables are soft with the shuffle and snorts of horses. They watch me from their sideways eyes, their lashes long and beautifully curled. "Hello again," I say with a lame wave. "Do you remember me? I came here and brought your human back to the city."

No response, but that's probably not the way to win them over.

I walk past a gorgeous ebony horse who reminds me of the book *Black Beauty.* And a smaller chestnut brown with long hair that seems to fall into his eyes. I don't actually know whether they're male or female, and it seems rude to try to peek. I didn't even buy them dinner first.

Gold Rush is in the last stall, standing as far away from the door as she can. Her beautiful white-beige mane shines in the faint morning light. Her eyes are a pale color too, a sort of gray that seems to go on for miles. "You really are beautiful," I tell her, a little wistful. "I can't be too mad at Sutton for coming to visit you, can I?"

She shakes her head, a little show of defiance at me for speaking.

"I bet you give him a hard time when he's been gone too long, don't you? The cold shoulder. Make him really work for it. I feel you, sister. You and me both."

The stall next to hers is empty, which I think might not be an accident. She's wary around humans, I already know, but is she also nervous around horses? Probably, which makes me terribly sad. To be isolated from everyone, even your own kind. It's a goddamn tragedy.

I take a step closer to the door, muscles tense in case I need to jump away. "Do they judge you for being different?" I whisper. "Do they wish you would be obedient like they are?"

Her foreleg lifts and then stomps lightly, sending up a small cloud of dust.

"They don't understand," I say. "Do they? They don't know why you fight it so hard."

She takes a step toward me, and I hold my breath, waiting for something violent. Something wild. Except she only stretches her neck toward me. Softly, softly. I hold my hand out, unwilling to reach past the door. I'm right on the edge, waiting.

Her breath whooshes against my palm.

"Get away from her."

The strident command makes Gold Rush pull away with an indignant snort, and I jump back in surprise. Sutton is only a dark shadow against the backdrop of sunrise. Hurt clenches my chest, and I take a step back nice and slow. "Are you avoiding me?"

A pause while he crosses the stable to stand beside me. He comes into focus in parts—his golden hair, his tanned skin. His blue eyes. They look hard this morning. "No."

Except the reserve in his expression wasn't there last time I saw him. He *is* avoiding me. "You said you weren't mad at me," I whisper, regret a cold rock in my throat.

"Is that what you think this is? Some kind of revenge bullshit?"

"Not when you put it that way. But I don't know what else it could be." I don't know how else to reconcile the charming man who pushed me up against the wall of L'Etoile with the man who had sex with me and then immediately left. The man who sat in my kitchen with a warm smile and then left town to avoid me.

He swears softly, turning away toward the

back door of the stable, where a honeycomb of pastures begins. "You shouldn't have come here. And you sure as hell shouldn't go near Gold Rush. Not anywhere near her stall."

"Because she's been neglected?"

"Because she's dangerous."

"Maybe she'll get socialized faster if you don't put her in the corner."

"Yeah? Or maybe she'll kick hard enough to break the door down."

"Why are you being so hard on her?"

"Why do you care?" His tone is cold enough to freeze me where I stand, but I have a lot of experience dealing with assholes. I fell in love with one when I was sixteen.

"Because you're doing the same damn thing to me that you did to her, putting her away when it gets hard, telling yourself that you're doing it for her own good."

He takes a step closer to me, his silence heavy. "It's not you," he says, and I shake my head.

"Don't lie to me."

"It's not *only* you." He looks more than pissed off; he looks shaken. As if my presence here bothers him on a bone-deep level. As if talking about this reaches to the core of him.

"What the hell is going on, Sutton? This is

more than competition between two alpha males, isn't it? I know it is. You're hiding something."

He turns away from me, proving the point. "It's none of your business."

A few steps and I plant myself in front of him again. "You had your cock inside me a few weeks ago. You played with my clit while you groaned my name. This is totally my business."

His low growl reaches into my chest. "You could have said no."

"I wanted you then." I take a step closer, enveloped in the scent of earth and sweat and sex. "And I want you now. I think you want me too."

An uneven laugh. "I look at you and I'm hard. You give me attitude, and I'm like goddamn iron. There's about a hundred ways I want you, and when we're done with that, I'll think up a hundred more."

He doesn't take a step toward me. Doesn't move a muscle. "What's stopping you?"

"And when you're done fucking around with me?"

I flinch at the word *fucking*, the way it's laced with accusation. The way he makes it sound hollow. Isn't he right? It's not like we're married, riding off into the sunset on three of his horses. We had a threesome after an illegal poker game.

"Don't tell me you found religion."

Another low sound, this one menacing. He does move then, pushing me back, crowding me against slats of wood. "You don't have one goddamn idea what I believe."

"Then tell me," I challenge, pushing back, my palms against his chest. They don't move him any, but they give me an excuse to touch him. To measure him. To feel the muscles he's holding in check.

He dips his head near mine. "You're not the only one I dream about."

My body responds to the seductive timbre in his voice, which is sad, really sad, because he must be in love with someone else. At least in lust with someone else. "Another woman?"

"No, sweetheart."

I pull back, staring hard at those beautiful blue eyes. "You're not—But he—"

"Go ahead and say it," he says in a drawl. "Spell it out for the horses, here. They don't understand."

My cheeks feel warm. I've turned over every rock, searching, demanding answers, and now that they're exposed to the sun, I'm suddenly worried. "You don't have to tell me."

"Oh, I think I do. After all I had my cock

inside you not long ago. I played with your clit while I groaned your name. Isn't that what you said?"

I swallow hard. "You… and Christopher?"

"No," he says sharply. "Don't get the wrong idea. We're not an item. Never have been. Never will be."

"But you want to be," I whisper. "Does he know?"

A rough sound. "Does he know? I don't even fucking know half the time. It's a goddamn mystery. A riddle designed to drive me slowly insane. It's un-fucking-knowable."

All the pain inside him pours out. It's always been there, simmering around him. Disguised as Southern charm, when really he's caught in unrequited love. Unrequited desire?

"All this time," I say, slowly wondering. I'm not hurt by this revelation, but there's time for that later. "When you wanted me. It's because of my connection to Christopher. When you took me to the theater, when you knelt down in front of me at L'Etoile. When you first saw me in your office."

"No. Yes. Hell, I'm not lying to you. You take over every room that you walk into. I knew there was something special about you from the way

Christopher talked, and then when I met you, it was over."

"What does that mean?"

"It means it doesn't matter whether I wanted to use you to get back at Christopher. Or to get close to him. When I saw you, when I got to know you, I fell for *you*, not for who you were to him."

"Oh, and you just magically got over him?"

"No," he says, as solemn as I've ever seen him. "I wish it were that simple."

I let my hands fall to my side, away from him. The loss feels like a physical blow. "You never really wanted me. Tell me the truth, Sutton. I deserve that much."

Something dark moves beneath those blue eyes. "Christ. Want you? I didn't want you, sweetheart. It was a craving. A need. Do you know how much it tore me up?" His voice comes out ragged, a man at the end of his rope. "I've spent the past six months trying to get you out of my head."

"Did it work?"

His gaze doesn't leave mine. "I wake up hard every morning, your taste on my tongue."

"It's as close as you'll ever get to Christopher Bardot. Is that it?" My voice is taunting because

I'm too shaken up. Too aware that I was between these men, both physically and emotionally. "You really want to suck his dick, but I'm the one who got to do it."

He grabs my hand and presses it against his jeans. The denim is well-worn from washing. I can feel him hard and impossibly hot. "This feel like I don't want you?"

I squeeze gently, and he makes a sound low in his throat.

"Go back to Tanglewood," he says, a little breathless.

He's thick and ready in my hand. I could push down my skinny jeans and turn around. He would be inside me in a matter of seconds. We would fuck like animals in this barn, but what would happen next? We'd have to face the reality that he wants Christopher.

And maybe I'd have to face the reality that I want Christopher, too.

I take a step back.

His blue gaze takes in every inch of me. I'm standing in the most unsexy pose in the history of the world, but he looks appreciative. My clothes might as well be see-through. There's a world of promise in that gaze. And for maybe the first time since his revelation, I think he might have been telling the truth about wanting us both.

All this time I wondered whether it was possible for me to love two men. The complexity of that. The pain of it. And Sutton had been struggling with his own impossible choice.

CHAPTER EIGHTEEN

FOR YOUR ENTERTAINMENT

I'M NOT COMPLETELY clueless when it comes to boys.

Sometimes it feels that way when I'm torn between Christopher and Sutton, when I'm a small boat tossed between an unforgiving night and stormy seas. But I used to give excellent advice when it came to boys. Everyone at Smith College came to me with questions—both the girls and the boys. Gay, straight, bisexual, whatever. I'd only ever had my fingers between my legs, never a man, but that didn't matter. I still knew the way boys thought. I knew what made them tick. I predicted their next move before they even figured it out.

But I had no idea that Sutton was interested in Christopher all along.

Had I been blind because I wanted Sutton to

be interested in only me? Or had he really buried the feelings down so deep that they were almost invisible? It makes me wonder what else I've been missing.

Well, maybe that's the difference.

I'm not completely clueless when it comes to boys, but Christopher and Sutton—they aren't boys. They're men. And I'm finding them as mysterious as living, breathing surrealist art.

Yes, Daddy made me cynical about men. Maybe my mother did that too, marrying so many rich assholes after him. I assume the worst about them, but they just keep proving me right. Even Christopher, which breaks me anew every single time. Who puts me back together with those rare moments of tenderness.

Around eight o'clock there's a knock on my front door. I open the door, ignoring the sense of relief that at least I guessed this part correctly. A mysterious man, a tormented man, but still a man.

Sutton fills the doorframe, his body ridiculously handsome in a thin T-shirt that hugs his arms and falls loose at his waist. And the torn jeans that have no right to look that sexy.

His face is in shadows, but I feel the torment radiating from him. "Can I come in?" he asks, a little gruff. I've seen him in a business suit making decisions around a conference table. I've seen him with his sleeves rolled up and a hard hat on, giving orders to a construction crew. There are a hundred ways he shows his strength, but he's never seemed as masculine as he does now—when he's achingly vulnerable to me.

"Is this a booty call?" I ask, hand on my hip.

He looks down at the row of pumpkins, each featuring a different-shaped cock. There's long and short, thick and curved. "Is that what you want?"

"A bunch of cocks?" I glance back to where *Casablanca* plays on the TV. Mom fell asleep before the French national anthem drowned out the German soldiers. "Maybe it's what you want. We should call Christopher so you can have a good time."

The words are a challenge, and Sutton responds with a small laugh. "Call whoever you want, sugar. But don't pretend it's because you don't want him."

I reach for his wrist, ignoring the spark when we touch, ignoring the play of tendon and muscle within my grip as I pull him inside. "Oh, come in."

He leans back against the door after he closes

it. His arms cross, which make them bulge in a way that's hard not to admire. "Where did you see all those, anyway? I know you were a virgin when Christopher fucked you."

"There's lots of different kinds of experience," I say in a haughty voice, as worldly as Ingrid Bergman on the big screen. She was a lover to one man and married to another, a feat she managed with total grace. I bet she never wondered if she was going insane.

Sutton doesn't look convinced, so I admit, "Naked models in art class. They aren't really supposed to be erect, but someone would usually tell dirty jokes until they got hard."

"It was you, wasn't it?"

"Okay. Yes. *God.*"

His lips quirk. "And I bet they went home and jacked off all night long."

I can't help but dip my gaze to the bulge in his jeans, the denim worn around the edges. My breath hitches as I remember what he felt like inside me. He makes a growling sound. "If you look at me that way, I'm going to do something about it."

My feet back up before I can plan a retreat. Apprehension and desire war in my body. "Mom's not in bed yet. We're watching a movie."

His eyes don't leave mine. "I can wait."

That's what I'm worried about. I've never met a man with more patience. More determination. And it's scary, because I can feel my defenses crumbling every second. Only I'm not sure what he's fighting for—Christopher or me.

Or maybe some combination that can never come true.

SUTTON HELPS ME wake up Mom, who says she hadn't actually slept for an hour of the movie. She insists on playing cards with Sutton, who agrees with an easy smile. I make hot cocoa for everyone—extra marshmallows for Sutton—while my mother wins three rounds of gin.

It's almost possible to believe she isn't sick until it's time for her to go to sleep. Then I help her walk up the stairs because she's too weak to climb them herself. I tuck her into bed like she's a child, because it's one of the only things I can do.

There is an assortment of herbal medicines I hand her, one after the other. The only prescription medicine she allows is something that helps her sleep.

"That Sutton is a nice man," she says, her voice soft. "Not like your daddy."

Acid burns my throat because I think she's right.

And because I think she's wrong.

He's not mean like Daddy, but even Daddy was nice once. He had been in love with the woman who now looks so frail beneath the pin-tuck comforter. It was his own ambition that made everything terrible, and both Sutton and Christopher have plenty of ambition.

A feeling of melancholy settles over me like falling leaves on the front lawn.

Downstairs I find Sutton with a bottle of wine and two glasses. That's how we end up in front of the fireplace, my toes warm from the gas fire. The scent of pine cones fills the air—an affectation from the expensive fake log. It's not exactly a rustic scene, but it pretends to be one.

"So what's the deal with your not-sister?" I ask, taking a sip of wine.

"My what?"

"The woman I met at your ranch earlier this year."

"Ah." He stares into the fire, his jaw square and shadowed. "I already told you I worked on a ranch. My daddy was a drunk and a bastard, but he had a way with horses, which is why they kept him around as long as they did."

How many frat boys have I sat with, taking confessions from them like I'm some kind of female priest? Never has it been as important to me as now, never have I strained forward, hungry for every word out of his mouth.

"He had a way with women, too. Slept with most every woman in a hundred miles, despite the fact that he had no money and not a speck of kindness."

If he had half his son's good looks, it didn't exactly surprise me. Those blue eyes could charm anyone into anything… in my case, they charmed a virgin into a threesome. "You hated him."

"Everyone hated him, but no one more than me. There were all these blue-eyed kids. People whispered about it. But in the end they got to live somewhere else. I was the only one stuck with him."

"I'm sorry."

"Hell… I don't… It's old news around here. Everyone knew about it. Except maybe Whitney. She was younger than me. Maybe people were more careful about what they said around her."

"And she had a crush on you?" It's disturbing enough to have a crush on my stepbrother; I know what that's like. But it would be way more disturbing to have had a crush on an actual blood relative. That would be hard to live down.

"I tried to discourage her without telling her. In the end it was some kid at school who gave her the bad news, and by then she was humiliated. Didn't speak to me for a year. She forgave me in the end, but it was unfortunate."

"You probably just… made her feel safe. When you're young, that feels like love."

"The ranch was worn at the edges when I worked there. By the time I grew up, her daddy had died and the place was in debt. It was the first property I ever bought."

"Not the last."

He comes to stand in front of me. "The library was the last."

Only a foot of air separates us now. I have to look up to meet his gaze. "Christopher has a way of ruining a person, doesn't he? You meet him and boom, it's all over."

That earns me a faint smile. "You're pretty destructive yourself."

I place my palm on his chest, feeling the steady rise of his breath, the beat of his heart. "You feel nice and solid. Put together. Not broken at all."

"A trick of the light," he says softly, blue eyes intent on mine.

"Have you told him?" I whisper because confessions can't come too loud.

A slow shake of his head. He retreats to the armchair opposite mine. "What would I say? He makes me want to punch him in the face. He makes me want to climb out of my skin. There's not a word for what I feel when he's in the room."

"Desire?"

"The closest thing would be... maybe obsession. The most unhealthy, fucked-up kind of obsession. It made me throw my money in with his. Made me go after the woman he loves."

Obsession. "Do people ever just meet and fall in love and get married?"

That earns me a soft laugh. "I'm sure you've met plenty of well-adjusted guys in college. Why aren't you married to one of them already?"

"I don't know," I say, but that's a lie. I wanted magic and fireworks and the kind of explosive chemistry that changes my DNA. It makes me sound too naive to admit that.

"I'll tell you why. Because none of them could have kept up with you, none of those pumpkin cocks would have been enough."

His words echo on my skin with total truth.

Those frat boys who brought me lukewarm beer in a plastic cup, the ones who lured me into an upstairs bedroom only to collapse into confessions at the slightest sign of kindness. They couldn't have handled the real me, and the thought gives me a sense of power. A sense that, amid my confusion and doubt, I'm in the right place.

I'm wearing jeans and a T-shirt, my makeup smudged after a long day, drops of water on my shirt from helping my mother shower before bed. This is the least sexy I've ever been, but I become a siren right here in this armchair. I'm a seductress for the ages as I stand up in front of Sutton. His blue eyes darken, proving me right, goading me on.

It doesn't really matter what I look like, anyway. I'm burned out on grief, desperate to feel something real. Maybe I want Christopher, but so does Sutton.

All we have in this moment is each other.

"What are you doing?" he asks, sounding amused. "Do you want a new model for your pumpkins? Because I have to tell you, I'm not going to stand very still like the boys at art school. I'm not going to get hard for your entertainment."

"No?" I ask, reaching for the hem of my T-shirt. I have on a plain white bra underneath, but it might as well be black silk for how proud I feel once I'm bared. "But I would heckle you so nicely. And I think you'd enjoy it, Sutton, I really do."

A muscle ticks in his jaw. "You are playing with fire."

"Sometimes a girl wants to get burned." I push my jeans down my hips and step out of them, revealing plain pink panties that are soft from washing a hundred times, and he sucks in a breath. He's already hard, judging from the way the denim stretches taut between his legs. He's tense everywhere, muscles flexing in his arms, his thighs. His whole body held at alert.

His voice is hoarse. "If I get up from this chair I'm going to have you bent over the side of the couch so fast you'll get dizzy. I won't bother taking off your panties, I'll push them out of the way so I can get inside you. I'll reach under your bra and touch your breasts, pinch your nipples until your tight little pussy squeezes around my cock."

Now it's my turn to squirm, legs pressing together where I stand. My body aches for what he promises, but I don't want to lose control of the situation. "You aren't allowed to get up from that chair. Those are the rules."

"Never been real good at following rules, sugar."

"Does that mean you can't handle me? I thought you were stronger than those frat boys."

A low chuckle. He stands up with slow, deliberate movements. And he pulls his shirt off the same way, revealing ridges of well-defined abs and a landscape of tanned skin. "I'm plenty strong, but I think you know that. Strong enough to see through your rules bullshit."

My mouth feels dry. There's a jump in my heartbeat that reminds me of holding my hand out to Gold Rush, feeling her breath against my palm. Having so much violence so barely restrained. There's no wooden door between me and the animal in front of me now.

"Strong enough to give you exactly what you want, even if you're going to fight me." He opens the placket of his jeans, revealing his bare cock. No underwear or boxers between the rough denim and his flesh. He's hard and thick and shiny at the tip. He runs a cruel fist down the length of his erection, twisting at the top as if he needs to hold something off.

Even if you're going to fight me. The crazy thing is, even I don't know if I'm going to fight him. The way he looks at me makes me wet and pliant. My fear makes me stiff. I take a step back. "I'm allowed to say no, Sutton."

"You're allowed to. Maybe I'll even believe you."

And then he would leave me here, all worked up with nothing but my pumpkin cocks to satisfy me. "You really do want me," I say, my gaze flicking from his hard cock to his intense eyes. "I'm not just a Christopher stand-in."

He laughs, though there's no humor in it. "Oh, sugar. You have no idea. I would fuck you all night long, even if I never saw Christopher again. I would fuck you for the rest of my life if you let me. You're the one using me as a stand-in."

The idea makes me gasp, but there's no time to dwell on it. No time to think about whether I would really do that. No time to wonder why, because Sutton always keeps his promises. He flips me around and has me bent over the curved arm of the sofa. My body arches as he touches two fingers to my most sensitive place. Arousal gives him all the slickness he needs. It's my own desire that betrays me, letting him invade me. Then his cock nudges me, burning hot.

I arch my back, though I don't know whether

I'm asking him to wait or wanting him to do it harder. Faster. Deeper. Then he slides inside, and it's like I'm complete. My body had been hurting from the space inside it, and now he's there—filling me almost like he belongs there. It's the fake pine cone scent from the logs, a way to pretend this is real.

He cups my breast through the white bra, and I flinch away, already knowing what comes next. He told me, didn't he? He told me how the story went, but still I find it shocking when he presses my nipple between thumb and forefinger, when he sends a bite of pain through my breast.

"I'm not," I gasp between the first thrust and the second, my eyes shutting tight against the pleasure so sharp it turns to pain. "Not. Not. Not."

"Not what?" he murmurs, pressing deep for a long moment.

I'm not using him as a Christopher stand-in, at least I don't think so. And I don't think he's using me, either. "I'm not in love with Christopher Bardot."

"You keep telling yourself that." A hard thrust. Another. "You keep saying it."

I don't know whether he means it literally, but that's what I do. I say it out loud, over and over. "I'm not in love with... not in love with Christopher... Oh God, Christopher Bardot!"

He finds my clit, merciless with two rough fingers, making me flinch. "Say it again."

"I'm not," I sob, but it feels more and more like a lie.

Sutton bites down on my shoulder, and the bright-hot pain is enough to shatter me. A low keening sound fills the room, the sound of my longing, the terrible pleasure I take from it—and behind me, the agonized groan of a man pushed past reason. His hips press against mine, hard enough I have to gasp for breath, my mouth open against the embroidered fabric of the sofa, hands clenching at nothing, his tongue laving the teeth marks he left on my skin.

In the aftermath we collapse in a heap, the sofa giving a slight shift of discomfort under our combined weights. Sutton moves when I'm still boneless, lifting himself off me and turning me over. His hands are gentle as he pulls on my clothes. It's like he's mourning something.

"We should talk. Tomorrow at the library. We'll talk then."

I stop him, my hand clasping his. "Stay."

He doesn't look broken, but I've learned that it's a beautiful facade. The intimacy we shared pulled down the walls, if only for a few seconds. Those calloused hands, so strong and sure with a dangerous horse, they're shaking. He needs the comfort of welcoming arms as much as I do.

And so I lead him back to the sofa, where we fall into a sudden and boundless sleep, our limbs tangled together, taking solace in a shared desperation.

CHAPTER NINETEEN

HONEST TO A FAULT

I N MY DREAM there are piles of straw, mountains of it, and no matter how hard I try, I can't spin them into gold. My fingers are torn up from the attempts, bloodied and raw. There's a lock on the door and a faint lightening of sky through the bars, which means the king will expect me to be done spinning soon. I'm running out of time.

I wake up with a sudden start, my eyes wide open as I look around the living room. A knock comes at the door, and I realize that must have woken me up. My palms are pressed to a chest as wide and solid as a table, but rising and falling in gentle breaths. Sutton looks up at me, rather adorable in his sleepy state. "You expecting someone?" he says, his voice rusty.

A glance at my phone. Four thirty. In the

morning.

I pull open the door, half expecting there to be some kind of overly polite burglar. Who else shows up at four thirty? Christopher Bardot, apparently. He doesn't even have the grace to look sleepy. Instead he leans casually against the doorjamb, one hand in the pocket of worn gray sweatpants. His white T-shirt looks like it's been washed a million times and probably feels like heaven. I have no doubt that he stepped out of bed looking like this, which is proof that the universe is fundamentally unfair. My eyes feel bloodshot, the place between my legs sore.

"I hope there's a bullet wound under that crisp white shirt," I tell him, my voice dark with exhausted aggravation. "Because I can't think of any other reason you'd be here at this time."

"We have to talk."

"About the meaning of life? About the birds and the bees? What could you possibly have to say to me at four thirty in the freaking morning that couldn't wait for six hours?"

"It's about the library. You can't fix it."

"Oh God, not this again."

"The building isn't fucking stable."

"You're not stable," I say, knowing full well that I sound like a five-year-old. But it's really early. Or late, depending on how you count it. All I know is that I've had about two hours of sleep. "Why don't you just build your little skyscraper and pretend the library doesn't exist?"

"I wish I could," he says grimly.

I feel the heat of Sutton's body before I hear him. "What's going on?"

Christopher's eyes darken. "What the hell is he doing here?"

Guilt shoots through me, which is seriously unfortunate because I don't owe Christopher Bardot any explanations. My body doesn't understand that. My body thinks it owes many things, and it decides to enumerate them using my imagination. "We're braiding each other's hair, and later we're going to use my Ouija board. What do you think he's doing here?"

"Harper, you can't believe everything he tells you." Christopher looks like he wants to say more, but he presses his lips together and looks away. "Hell."

Sutton holds my hips in a possessive and challenging gesture. "That's convenient coming from you. I think you're the one she shouldn't believe."

"God," I say, sleep clearing from my eyes. "You two just want to growl over me. It could be anything between you. I'm like a scrap of meat, and you're just hungry."

"You like it when I'm hungry," Sutton says, placing an openmouthed kiss to the side of my neck. He pulls one hand up until it rests under my breast. The other curves around to the lower plain of my belly, right above my sex. It's an incredibly intimate way to touch me, and I'm standing in the front door backlit by a soft lamp from inside.

Christopher's jaw works. His whole body looks tense, a spring pressed down into its smallest form, vibrating with the force to keep it that way. What would he do if he unleashed that power? Would he attack Sutton with blind rage? Or would he take it out on me in sensual torment, like he did at the Den? I'm holding my breath, and I can't deny that I hope for the latter. The three of us together are dysfunctional and wrong, but it feels so good.

"You want her?" Sutton asks gently, and I think he's pushing. Not only for sex. He's pushing until Christopher breaks. Until there's no hope of them together.

And maybe I'm doing the same thing.

Sometimes the Death Plan isn't printed in black-and-white. Sometimes it's whispering to us in the middle of the night. Sometimes it's leaning back against Sutton's body, knowing it will make Christopher come closer. His lips part, looking full, almost swollen as he watches us from beneath heavy lids. What would he say if he saw us bent over the sofa?

I'm not in love with Christopher Bardot.

Fear squeezes my throat. I'd rather push him away than watch him leave. "Come inside," I say with a patently fake smile. "It's more fun with both of you."

Christopher turns away from us, and I realize this hurts just as much. *You can't avoid this forever.* I break away from Sutton's hold and run after him. "Wait."

He stops a foot away from his car, still looking away. His body is held rigid, emanating intense emotion without moving a muscle. "You shouldn't trust him."

"You used to tell me that I shouldn't trust you either."

"That's true, too. Leave the both of us. Go back to New York. LA. Anywhere but here."

"I can't do that." I can tell myself that it's the library that keeps me here, but I have a growing suspicion that it's the man in front of me. If he went to Tokyo, I'd probably have to protest to save the cherry blossoms. It's a terrible weakness in me, this feeling.

"Or make him tell you the truth."

That makes me smile, though it's a little sad. "Do *you* know the truth?"

"What are you talking about?"

Sutton's obsession might not be one-sided. In that case I could be the one who brings them together. And then the one that's left standing as they ride off into the sunset. "I didn't think you were a coward, Christopher Bardot. To want someone and not tell them."

His eyes narrow. He reaches for me before I can blink, turning me before I can breathe, backing me up against the dew-dropped surface of his Tesla. "You want a declaration, Harper?"

This close I can see little silver flecks in his black eyes. How have I never noticed them before? He looks pissed off and wild, like a powerful animal that has suddenly found itself in an ironclad cage. He looks afraid, and I'm suffused with a sense of wonder. What could scare this man? Nothing, I would have said. But I would have been wrong. "Do you have anything to declare?" I whisper, a little mocking.

He leans forward, his lips an inch from my cheek. "Who's the coward now?" he murmurs against my temple, brushing a kiss so light it's like air.

What would bravery look like right now? No, I'm not very courageous. There's curiosity inside me, to see Sutton and Christopher together now that I know the feelings underneath. And there's my own growing unrest. Sometimes you have to break something in order to fix it.

"Come inside," I say, holding out my hand.

Sutton looks more surprised than me to see Christopher. As if pushing and pushing had been an archaic kind of mating ritual, one so ineffective that he had resigned himself to it never working. I have to face the facts—there is a chance that Christopher has buried feelings for Sutton, too. That I will lose both of them tonight. But I'm not going to hide in the shadows any longer. Not going to wait and wait and wait for these men to decide. I'm making the decisions right now, and I want them both in my bed.

The living room smells like warmth and roasted pumpkin seeds and sex. Sutton's shirt is slung over the armchair. The cushions on the sofa are smooshed and rumpled from our bodies. It could possibly feel like a scene of guilt, of shame, and maybe when there was first a knock on the door it did.

Now it feels like Sutton and I are doing something together, like we've created this on purpose—the purpose being to seduce Christopher Bardot. It's working, if the clench of his jaw is anything to go by. And the bulge against his jeans.

"Upstairs." I mean to say it hard, like a command, but it comes out breathy. Both men follow me anyway, silent and large and looming on the sweeping staircase. It feels like I'm Little Red Riding Hood with two wolves prowling behind me, wondering which one will eat me first.

There's always the chance they'll eat each other.

My room has the flowered bedspread and antique dresser that was here when we moved in. There are no pictures on the side table, no modern art hanging on the wall. That's a good thing. It makes this more like a hotel room, which is where we first consummated our threesome.

"Where do you want me?" Christopher asks, and I have to acknowledge how truly weird this is. There are two men in this room with me. This may not be the first time we've been together, but it feels so strongly like the last.

"On the bed," Sutton says, his voice soft and supple like worn leather.

"I asked Harper," Christopher says, diamond eyes flashing.

"And I'm telling you what she wants. Or can't you tell? Can't you see how wet she gets when you look at her that way, all cold and mean? It turns her on."

Except how could Christopher have seen that. Even I couldn't see that, and it's my body. Now that Sutton has said the words, I can't unsee it. I can't unfeel it. The only thing I can focus on is the way my nipples feel against my shirt, like a thousand nerve endings against sandpaper. The only thing I can see is the cruel twist to Christopher's lips. My body feels molten inside; he did that to me.

Christopher doesn't break eye contact as he sits on the edge of the bed. Such an innocuous thing to do, sit on the edge of a bed with all your clothes on. There's nothing inherently explicit about the act, but there's a livewire in my brain. A livewire that jolts me so hard and painful, because we're going to have sex. One thing is very different from the time at the poker game—this time I know how Sutton feels.

He looks the same as he always does, smug and laconic and a little too casual to be true. He takes a step toward Christopher, careful, careful, and I'm reminded of the way he approached Gold Rush. Affecting a calm that he didn't quite feel, pretending that he wasn't one hard kick away from having his skull bashed in. Sutton is good at pretending.

Except that Christopher does not appear fooled.

He stares hard at Sutton in that calculating way, as if adding up the cards and realizing there's one he missed. A notch forms between dark eyebrows.

"What about you?" he asks quietly. "Does it turn you on, too?"

Sutton flinches. "This isn't about me."

Black eyes flash. "I've played cards with you enough times to know your tells. And that one was a goddamn red flashing light. You want to say something to me?"

A dark laugh. "There's nothing to say."

Sexual violence rolls through the room, as heavy and electric as stormclouds. This could break out into a fight. Or it could break out into sex. I know which one I'd rather have.

"You," I murmur to Sutton. "I want you on the bed."

He looks at me like an animal backed into a corner, the whites of his eyes almost showing.

"I'm supposed to do what you say. I'm supposed to trust you."

That makes me smile. "I've trusted you plenty. Was I supposed to do that?"

A low growl. If there were fur on him, it would rise at the back of his neck. There's practically a snarl on his handsome face. It's hard to imagine that he's the softer of the two men right now. He looks feral. But he walks toward the bed. He sits down.

"All the way." My voice comes out hard. I think maybe he likes me hard.

He scoots back, his gaze promising retribution. "What next?"

I pretend to think about that, even though the vision is in my head clear as day. Clear as the feel of Sutton against my back and Christopher at my front. I have been between those two men in multiple ways, but never the one we're going to do tonight.

"Come here," I say to Christopher, a little shy.

It's easy to be the strong, seductive woman with Sutton. That's the only way he's ever seen me. Christopher has seen me young and stupid. He's seen me in love.

He tears his gaze from Sutton, uncertainty in his dark eyes. The question hovers on his lips, almost visible in the space between us. *Is this more than a rivalry between Sutton and me? Is this lust? Does Sutton want to fuck me? Do I want to fuck him back?*

"Yes," I say, my voice soft and coaxing. "Or no. Those are your options."

A faint smile. "You want to be in charge."

"Maybe, but you definitely want me to be in charge."

"Yeah," he says, a low rumble.

This isn't the time for talking about feelings. What would Sutton say?

The most unhealthy, fucked-up kind of obsession.

No, this is only something that can be felt. The way that works with Gold Rush in that corral, both gentle and firm. The way he has to break her to make her trust again.

Christopher comes to me, a little wary. Even when I order him around, he's still tall enough that I have to look up. He gazes down at me with an impassive expression. Only the faint tremor running through his hard body gives him away. He wants this. Whatever wild thing happens next, even if it involves the bristling man on the bed.

I reach up and lick the corner of Christopher's lips. He sucks in a breath.

"How are you doing this?" he asks, but I'm

not sure what he means. Ordering two men around? By giving them what they secretly want, that's how. Even if they want each other.

Even if I'll be left alone in this room after.

My hands go to Christopher's shirt, pulling it up to reveal his abs with slow precision. I could be performing surgery, that's how careful I am right now. I could be cutting out my own heart with a goddamn scalpel. His chest looks bronze in the moonlight, like he's forged and molded. Like he's hollow inside. Except he's warm to the touch. I press my palm against his chest and feel the steady beat of his heart.

He's the one who moves to his pants, his gaze never leaving mine, as if obeying some unspoken command. *Undress*, I could have said to the most severe man I've ever met. He pushes down his sweatpants and kicks them off, revealing the hard length of him.

Only our breathing can be heard after that.

His pants are open, slack. He's so put together. It's a privilege to see him like this, coming apart. His hand twitches when I reach for him— maybe to stop me. Maybe to pull me closer. In the end he leaves his arms at his side. I run a finger down the center of his chest, feeling the indent of muscle and flesh. The wiry hair at the base.

My fist closes around him.

"God," he groans, throwing back his head.

He's beautiful like this, but I can't look at him. I need to see what Sutton's doing. He doesn't disappoint. He has his jeans undone and shoved down his muscular thighs, his cock in hand. He's staring at Christopher's body, lips parted, eyes heavy.

This is a man getting his deepest wish, and it gives me a sense of power to be the one who can fulfill it for him. Even as Christopher bucks against my hand. "That's right," I whisper.

Christopher stares at me through slitted eyes, his lips pulled tight. "You want me to embarrass myself, is that it? This some kind of revenge fuck?"

This is the farthest thing from a revenge fuck. The exact opposite. I'm putting together something that I broke. The partnership between the men. Maybe more than a partnership.

"Would you mind?" I ask, a smile flickering at my lips.

"Fuck," he says, lean hips fucking my fist. "Christ. I wouldn't."

Seeing Christopher in command is enough to make me wet, but seeing him this way, surrendering—it's enough to make me want to weep. It's like having a star on my palm. I know I won't be able to keep it, but I'll stay very still to make this last.

I turn and climb onto the bed. When I glance back Christopher is looking at my ass, almost forlorn now that he's the only one standing. "Come here," I murmur.

He follows me, but I move back. He has to chase me on the king bed.

And then I'm pressed up against Sutton's body, his hard body jerking on impact, his cock like a brand through my dress at the back. Then Christopher is on me, his lips hard on mine, payback for the orders, punishing. His tongue pushes inside my mouth.

I want to be the calm and unaffected seductress, but my body is melting between these two men. It would be impossible not to melt. There's hardness behind me. Hardness in front. A slickness between my legs like a goddamn river, and Christopher knows it.

"Push your panties out of the way," he says against my lips.

There's a tight squeeze in my sex, a clench around nothing. "Why should?"

"Because I'll kiss your breasts, sweetheart.

Sutton will hold up your tits for me, and I'll suck your nipples. You'd like that wouldn't you? You'd come for me."

Oh God. I close my eyes. "It's not about me tonight."

A soft laugh. This isn't a man scared of what happens next. "It's always been about you, Harper. Now push your panties aside. Do it, or I'll fucking tear them."

My fingers are somehow between my legs. The placket of my panties is already damp. I hook two fingers against it and push it aside. On the backs of my knuckles I feel the burn and velvet of Christopher's cock. Then he's pushing inside, opening me wide, making me moan.

A low masculine sound fills the room, and I have to open my eyes.

Christopher's expression is hard with pleasure, only an inch away from Sutton's face. It's like Christopher is fucking Sutton, with me in the middle. I'm a conduit right now, the thrust of hips and cock pushing me back against another body. Both of them rocking and grunting and using me in the most carnal ways.

At first it seemed like Sutton and I were the ones seducing Christopher.

Now it's the other way around. Sutton is the

one being seduced.

He grasps my hips hard enough to leave bruises. "Ahh fuck," he says, his breath hot on my throat. "Fuck. Like that. Don't stop. Don't fucking stop."

His words spur Christopher to fuck me harder, and faster, and he doesn't stop.

Sutton's cock is only rubbing against my back, almost a juvenile comfort, but he sounds more turned on than I've ever seen. The most out of control. "Harper," he says, and it sounds like he's dying.

"Don't talk to her," Christopher says, baring his teeth.

The words are confusing until I feel Sutton buck against me. He likes being warned away. He called it *fucked up* and I think he's right about that. This isn't a normal kind of lust. *Obsession.* I turn my face and place an open-mouth kiss on Sutton's cheek.

A hand grasps my face and turns me back. "Me," Christopher says, almost primitive now. "You look at me. You fuck me. That's what you want, isn't it? Say it."

"I want you," I whisper, but I'm not giving in all the way. He made me work too hard to get his attention. He made me wait too long for even a speck of sexual interest.

He punctuates each of his words with a hard thrust. "You. Want. Me."

I close my eyes, but he doesn't let me keep them that way. A little shake. A particularly hard, angled thrust that makes me squirm against Sutton. His whole body turns taut behind me.

"Harper," Christopher says, but his voice doesn't sound as hard as before. He seems a little breathless. On the edge of something he can't quite hold back.

His fingers work their way down my stomach, into the slick space between us.

The press together around me clit, and I shoot up toward him. "Please."

An unsteady laugh. "You were right," he says, except he isn't talking to me. He's talking to the man behind me. "She is too tight. Are you going to help her?"

Sutton reaches around to stroke my breasts. To pinch my nipples.

To hold up my tits, the way Christopher said he would.

The warmth of Christopher's mouth makes me cry out and clench hard. His lips are only an inch away from Sutton's fingers. His chin is probably brushing him. Christopher closes his eyes in pure ecstasy, and I want to watch, I do, but he sucks, and I have to throw my head back onto Sutton's shoulder and moan in sensory overload.

Christopher moves to my other breast, flicking his tongue against me. Sutton doesn't hold me up for him this time. Instead he reaches a hand up to stroke down Christopher's temple, the gesture so tender it makes my eyes prick with tears. And I think we should talk, we should; except Christopher pinches hard around my clit, and then I'm coming, coming, bearing down on Christopher's cock, making him gasp and hold me tight, Sutton behind us moaning, *yes yes yes* as a warm spot spreads across my back.

IN THE AFTERMATH I mostly expect for Sutton to disappear. That's what he did after the poker game, and he was a lot less exposed then. *I can't do this,* he'll say, and leave the house. Except he sits on the edge of the bed, looking shaken.

It's Christopher who stands and puts his clothes back on. There is no visit to the bar to get us drinks this time around. He doesn't have some kind of post-sex bartender habit after all. Instead he seems actually pissed, which makes my stomach feel upside down.

"Christopher?" I say, my voice tremulous.

"Don't."

That makes me want to push harder. "Christopher, don't be mad at Sutton. It was my idea. This whole thing was my idea. I don't think Sutton even liked it to be honest—"

"That's you being honest?"

I fall silent, acutely aware of the damp spot on my back, the proof of how much Sutton liked it. "You liked it too," I finally say, pulling the sheet over my lap as a shield.

"Yes," he says simply.

"Do you think that you're—"

"Gay?" Christopher asks. "No, sweetheart. I like your pussy too much for that."

"It's possible to be bi."

"Is this sex education night at the St. Claire household? I know what it means to be bi. And I know what it means to be straight. I'm not really any of those things. I'm wasted over a single person, Harper. Over you."

Goose bumps rise on my skin. *Over you.* I want to believe him, but it's hard to be joyful when it looks like Sutton is crushed. When it looks like he's questioning his sexuality. "You never said that to me." It pisses me off, suddenly. "Why didn't you ever say that to me?"

"Because it wasn't something I could buy," he says, his voice grim. "And that's on me, for wasting the time I should have been with you. For letting you be with Sutton."

My eyes narrow. "For letting me? You don't own me, Christopher."

He doesn't argue the point, but he doesn't agree either. "You aren't gay," Christopher says, his voice thoughtful now. He looks at Sutton as if seeing him for the first time.

"So how do you explain what just happened?"

"Harper happened. It doesn't have to mean anything."

"That's the problem," Sutton says, his voice hard. "Maybe I want it to." He stands and leaves the room, grabbing his jeans as he goes. The space he sat on the bed is still depressed from his hard, muscled weight. There's no filling the space where he's been.

Christopher meets my gaze. "I'm done sharing you."

There's an ache in my chest. If he's done sharing me, does that mean he's done *having* me? I'm not sure if Sutton and I are a package deal.

"What does that mean?"

"Ask him about the library," he says, ominous.

"You're leaving?"

"I think he needs you more. Tonight."

I follow him down the stairs and watch him pull out of the driveway. Sutton comes to stand beside me, watching the corner where the red taillights disappeared. He looks broken, and I feel bad asking him when he's like this but I have to know. "The library."

He sounds almost absentminded. "What about it?"

"The foundation issues. The termites. The plumbing. Is it really fixable?"

"I said it was, Harper."

"So you're telling me the truth?"

Sutton looks behind us at the house. I'm not sure what he sees. Does he recognize the *Gone with the Wind* columns? Or does he only see a place with pumpkin-carved cocks and cookies inside? "Honest to a fault," he finally says. "That's me."

Then he lopes to his car, moving slowly like someone who's been delivered some fatal blow. As if Gold Rush kicked him in the ribs the last time I went, except I know he was uninjured only a few hours ago.

Sutton may have meant to push Christopher to his breaking point, but I think he found his own instead. He doesn't look back as he gets into his car and drives away. Only when I'm standing alone in the lightening sky does it feel like I might never see him again.

CHAPTER TWENTY

DEATH PLAN

"GRAHAM." MY MOTHER'S voice is thin as paper, as wavery as the wind.

I stroke her hair and she quiets. I came in to check on her after the men left, and she seemed fine. This morning everything changed. She barely woke up when I spoke to her, even though she's always been an early riser, doing her sun salutations every morning with a yoga mat on the porch. Her sessions have been shorter and shorter, but this morning she doesn't even get out of bed.

Guilt suffuses me as if somehow she's doing worse because I had such a great orgasm bent over the couch downstairs with Sutton last night. I don't know if the universe really works on such a terrible balance sheet, but if I learned anything from Daddy, it's that if you're losing, someone else is winning.

Mom shifts in her uneasy nap, her skin flushed. It seems unfair that she should still dream about Daddy when he humiliated her at the end. He knew the society wives would shun her after being publicly left out of his will. And here she is, missing him and in pain—I suppose those are the same things.

"Don't go, Graham. Don't."

A sharp pain in my heart. "Mom," I whisper. "Wake up."

Except I don't want her to wake up before it's time to give her another dose of meds. That was the only prescription she accepted from the doctors. They couldn't save her life, and right now they can't even keep her comfortable. The nurse showed up this morning and checked Mom's vitals, but I sent her back downstairs. If she's going to be hurting, the least I can do is sit with her.

A low moan comes from her throat, and she thrashes weakly in the thousand-count bedsheets. Not even money will save us in the end. I bend down low, murmuring in her ear, "He's not going anywhere, Mom. He loves you. He's right here, and he loves you."

Sometimes the truth isn't going to help you. Only lies will do that.

Her brow smooths out, and her breathing becomes even again. She's drifting off to sleep, but I keep running my hand over her hair. It feels light somehow, as if she's made of air, as if she'll blow away if I don't hold her here.

I must fall asleep because at a sudden sound I wake up. For a second, with one foot still in dreams, the other in a bleak reality, I think it's Christopher knocking on the door. Relief is cool and sweet through my body, a cube of ice at the base of my throat on a hot summer day. Then I realize it's not Christopher. There's no one at the door. It's my mother coughing, groaning—a terrible rattling sound that makes my heart beat double time. "Mom?"

There's no response, and I shake her, hard, too hard, need her to answer. "Mom! Wake up! I need you to wake up right now." I'm crying because the terrible sound doesn't stop, the rasping precursor to death. I knew this was coming. I should have been prepared for this, but I'm not. I'm not.

I'll never be ready to lose her.

I stare blankly at the still form under the covers, the sound of her sawing breath like a blade against my heart. The realization comes to me slowly, that she won't die this second. Or the next. The panic fades to a dull ache of grief. My hands are shaking as I find my cell phone in the mess of blankets, still warm from where I'd been sleeping, rumpled from where I'd startled awake.

The nurse is only downstairs, probably preparing a light lunch that my mother will never eat. In the same house, but I don't think I could yell for her. I can barely speak into my phone when she answers. "I think it's time."

The ambulance arrives without its lights flashing. This isn't an emergency. This has been painstakingly prepared. This is the Death Plan. The one I never could bear to read.

I guess I'll find out what it says.

Freida was right about that—I couldn't avoid it forever. She stands with me, holding my hand while the EMTs move my mother's still-breathing body onto the stretcher and into the ambulance. I follow them down the stairs, a cold sweat breaking out over my skin.

AVERY MEETS US at the hospital, which means Freida must have called her right after the ambulance. Part of the Death Plan, no doubt.

The plan that's supposed to make this easy. Or at least, not hard.

She grasps me in a hard hug that I barely feel. I'm going numb, the tips of my fingers already gone, a frost spreading from the outside in. "I'm so sorry," she whispers, squeezing tighter. It would probably hurt, but I'm too far gone. "What can I do, sweetie? We're here for you."

That makes me look up, and I see that Gabriel is with her, looking stern and faintly sympathetic, a dark slash of suit against the sterile white hospital backdrop. He gives me a nod, which makes me want to punch him in the face. Does he know how much Avery worried while he was gone? He should just have a heart attack right now and spare her the agony of a slow death later.

I'm being totally irrational, and I break out into tears on the shoulder of my old friend. "I'm sorry," I gasp, clinging to her. "I didn't mean it. I don't want Gabriel to have a heart attack."

Gabriel coughs. "I appreciate that," he says, his voice grave.

"Do you want to go sit down?" Avery asks. "Gabriel will make sure your mom has everything she needs. You should take a little break."

I shake my head, eyes closed tight. "The hospital already has the Death Plan."

Avery pulls back, her hazel eyes searching and sympathetic, not even a little bit jarred by the words *Death Plan*. "Do you want to talk about it?"

"Wait. Have you read the Death Plan?"

"Yes," she says, her voice overly reasonable. "I had a meeting with your mother."

"Is there a section titled *People To Console Harper*?"

"No." Her voice does a high-pitched thing at the end which means I hit close to the mark.

Footfalls approach from behind me, and I whirl around to face Sutton. He looks warm and empathetic, and I take a step back as he nears, bumping into Avery, afraid that he'll melt the ice around me, and then what would happen? I would feel everything. All the pain. All the loss. Those blue eyes hold a wealth of understanding. "I can go if you want," he says softly.

"No," I say even though I don't know what I want.

A good daughter would already know what's on the Death Plan. I should have been the one to call the ambulance and gather everyone. A good daughter would have forgiven her mother for being terrible at love, even though I didn't realize until this second how angry I was.

Why didn't she make it work with my father? Why did she have to choose someone so rich and emotionally unavailable in the first place? Why couldn't she ever settle down? Surely there was a man somewhere in the country who would have loved and cherished a beautiful woman, even if she would never be accepted by the rich society wives.

I had to experience love to understand the impossibility of it. I had to stumble so that I could forgive my mother for falling again and again. We don't mean to; we don't want to. The ground opens up underneath us, and there's nowhere to go but down.

"Where is it?" I say, my voice shaky but sure.

Sutton looks concerned. "Where's what?"

"The Death Plan. I need to see the Death Plan. I should have read it when she first asked me to, but it doesn't matter. The important thing is that I read it now."

A notch forms between Avery's eyebrows. "You don't need to worry about that," she says in what I assume is a soothing tone. "Freida and the hospital have everything taken care of."

"I still need to see it."

There is a grace in accepting defeat that I haven't acquired. I only know how to fight, how to protest, how to stage an event so big that an entire city bands together to save a library.

Right now I'm surrounded by the things my mother dislikes the most—the smell of antiseptic and doctors. Because she learned how to accept death with grace.

A piece of paper appears in front of me, a little crinkled from its journey, darkened spots appearing where my tears mar the ink. I struggle to hold it steady enough to read.

Now I understand how much bravery it took for her to write down what she wanted to feel, to hear, to see. Now I understand what it means to surrender—not weakness but strength.

I swallow hard, turning away from Avery and Gabriel.

Turning away from Sutton.

"Thank you for coming," I tell them because I feel an immense gratitude. And the incredible certainty that I'm going to be alone. "According to this we'll be here for some time… waiting. You don't have to wait here. I'm sure she didn't want that."

Which isn't exactly what the Death Plan says.

"Harper." Avery whispers my name, her voice pained.

She already knows what's on the paper. My

mother made sure that I wouldn't be alone for this. She knows I love Avery like a sister. And she knows I have feelings for Sutton.

"I'm not leaving you here," Sutton says because he doesn't know.

My throat aches. "Most of her organs are torn up by the cancer. But her eyes are fine. She's donating her corneas to someone who needs them."

"It's a good thing," Avery says, but she doesn't sound sure.

"It means she has to die in the hospital, because they have to remove them right away. So we have to stay here until it happens. It could take hours. Days. Weeks."

"Jesus, Harper." Sutton sounds angry, which strikes me as odd. Nothing much makes him angry, except maybe loving Christopher. "She's going to make you watch her die?"

That makes me turn to look at him, a sad smile turning my lips. "What do you think I've been doing? It started before I even came to Tanglewood, before I even saw the library—the cancer that would kill her. There was only one way for this to end."

The Death Plan requests the presence of Avery, of course.

And my friend Bea, who won't come because she can't.

It requests the presence of Sutton, who played gin over milk and cookies. These are all the people I love. And right there in black-and-white—Christopher Bardot, the man my father used to hurt her. Only now, as I stand in the overbright hospital hallway, do I fully realize what it cost her. Only now do I realize what she spent.

My mother's in that hospital bed. It's my personal rock bottom. I'm lying at the bottom of a pond, looking up at my reflection. And there's only one face I see.

One person I want by my side at the hardest moment of my life. He isn't here.

CHAPTER TWENTY-ONE
VITAL SIGNS

THE *BEEP-BEEP-BEEP* OF the machines drills into my head. It sinks into my soul until all I hear is the sound of beeping when I remember doing yoga with my mom in the mornings before school. Beeping when we watched old movies together. Beeping when I called her from Daddy's yacht and told her about Christopher for the first time. *Don't get too close,* she told me then. *It's only temporary.* I'm bloodshot by the time morning comes, splashing my face with water so I can see straight.

"Didn't you get any sleep?" Avery asks, gently admonishing. Gabriel insisted she go home at midnight, and I supported that. There was no reason everyone should have insistent beeps playing on a loop in their overtired brains, even when they go to the bathroom where it's quiet.

She bustles around with a calm I can only admire, setting down a fresh coffee in front of me. Picking up the ten thousand pieces of Styrofoam that I pulled apart from my last coffee.

She cared for her father when he was hurt.

"How did you do it?" I ask.

"The same way you are," she says. "I was strong when I had to be."

Except she also had to worry about paying the bills. And about someone wanting revenge on her family. About selling her virginity to the highest bidder. *God.* My problems are small in comparison, but looking at my mother in that hospital bed, so frail and tied up with tubes and wires she never wanted, I feel like I'm falling apart. "I don't feel strong."

A hand covers mine, squeezing softly. "It never feels that way when you're in it. And then you come out the other side and you realize that you survived."

"You mean when my mother's dead. That's what the other side looks like."

Her face falls. "I'm sorry."

"No." I turn my hand over to grasp hers. "I'm stressed, but I shouldn't take it out on you."

She's only trying to console me, but I won't let myself be consoled. I *can't* let myself be consoled at a time like this, because the pain is the only thing keeping me grounded right now.

There's a small voice in my head that says I'm more like my father than I ever want to admit. When things got hard, he left his wife and found a new one. He shipped his daughter back to boarding school. And he pushed away his wife and his daughter in his will. I'm sitting here in this cold, sterile room, and I don't know what the easy way out looks like right now—but the weak part of me wants it.

A nurse comes into the room, checks vital signs and adds a bag to the IV drip, her smile taut with the knowledge that there's nothing she can really do. We're all just waiting for someone to die so we can harvest her eyeballs. That's the grim reality of the Death Plan.

"When did Gabriel get back?" I ask because I feel like lashing out.

Because I can hurt my friend as much as I can hurt myself. She flinches. "A couple nights ago. I didn't want you to worry about me. You have enough going on."

There's a fracture in my heart. The hard stone is only a casing, and once it cracks, I'm back to being fully human. Fully vulnerable. "Oh, Avery. I'm so sorry."

"Don't," she whispers, fierce in her loyalty. That's Avery to the end.

"I should go punch him in the face. That's what I bring to the table. A fight. Except I don't know how to swing at a hungry cancer cell that's eating my mother. I don't know how to punish myself for being alive when she's so close to dying.

"You definitely shouldn't punch him in the face," she says with a sigh. "I just wish I knew what he wanted. He's right there, standing probably a few feet from the door, but he's so far away."

I rub my eyes, but they're filled with grit. "I know this is going to sound dumb but... did you ask him what the problem is? Like really ask him?"

"Yes," she says, but the word is drawn out as if maybe she didn't.

That makes me set down the cup of coffee. "Avery."

She looks guilty. "I *did* ask him, okay? I ask him almost every day over the phone if anything is bothering him, and he says *no*, or *just work*, or *is there something on your mind, Avery?* But then I'm afraid to say yes, afraid to push him that much farther, because what if I don't like what comes next?" Her voice drops to a whisper. "What if that's the end of us?"

Her hazel eyes are so hopeful, as if I might have the answer, but I've never been able to say things with words. That's why the library is both my foil and my greatest ambition, the thing just out of reach. "You know the first thing I learned as an artist?"

"That you're brilliant?"

"Hah. No. I had to learn about colors before I could make anything with them. If you want to make a color brighter, you put it next to its complementary color, its opposite on the color wheel. It doesn't actually change the color, but it looks that way."

"The fact that Gabriel and I worked well together was just an optical illusion?"

"But if you mix those complementary colors together, they create the darkest shadows."

She scrunches her nose. "Please tell me this analogy isn't about sex."

"Of course it's about sex. Art is always about sex. That's the second thing I learned as an artist."

"Only the second thing? Didn't you get into an exclusive summer program at the Harvard Art School when you were in middle school?"

"And I had this crush on Mr. Mendocino that gave me quite an education. The important thing is that complementary colors don't want to mix together. They want to be next to each other."

"You're saying that Gabriel is pulling back because we're getting too close?"

"No, Avery. I'm saying *you* are. You're determined to find something wrong, and I think it's because you're scared. Of what, I have no idea. He's a dangerous bastard, sure, but you knew that when he bid on your virginity, and you still fell in love with him."

Her eyes go bright with tears. "I do love him."

"I know," I say softly because I know she would do anything for the man standing outside. And he would do anything for her, including drive her to the hospital at five a.m. in the morning after leaving only a few hours before that. "What are you afraid of, Avery?"

"My dissertation is finished."

"Oh. That's good, right?"

"It's been finished. I told everyone I was taking the semester away from school to work on it, but it was done before I left. It was one thing to do the long-distance, constant-travel thing while I was in school, but Gabriel has a condo in Hong Kong and a building in Dubai, in addition to his mansion in Tanglewood. There are a million places he needs to be, but none of them are in a sleepy, snooty college town."

"Why would you be in a college town—Oh. You want to teach?"

"I don't have official offers right now, of course, but my advisor at Smith College is already begging me to stay. And I advised on this grant about Feminism and Families in the Trojan War at Berkley, and I would love to work with them."

"Oh, Avery. Do you think Gabriel wouldn't follow you there?"

"He would."

"Then what's the problem."

"That's just it. He would follow me someplace that isn't good for him, that wouldn't make him happy. And how do I know that? Because he isn't happy now, and he isn't telling me. What kind of future is that? Him getting quieter and quieter while I traipse around academia, doing whatever I want?"

"Honestly I love that you can call writing ten thousand pages on mythological ovaries *traipsing*, but I think you really need to talk to Gabriel. What if it's actually his greatest dream to live in a snooty college town, wearing a black turtleneck and sipping espresso with his pinky finger up?" At her dubious look, I say, "Okay, probably not. But I still think you should talk to him."

"I'll think about it," she says, but that probably means she's going to stare at him and sigh over him and then sacrifice what she loves so she can be with him. It's almost enough to make me mad, but the truth is, I don't know the answer. What if two people love each other but they want different things? What if love is nothing but an endless wheel of compromise?

What if they mix and mix and mix until both of them are shadows of their former selves?

I grab the chart at the foot of the hospital bed and flip to an empty page, scribbling down some notes. "Can you go home and get this stuff from the house? I need a change of clothes."

There's more than clothes on the list. A portable speaker. The latest copy of Mom's meditation magazine. All of it might actually get used in the next few hours, but that isn't the only reason I'm sending her. I need the steady *beep-beep-beep* as much as I despise it. I'm going insane in this room, a fast and efficient one-way trip to despair, and I don't need company for the ride. At least not in the form of a sweet, steady friend.

I wait until she's gone before I pull out my cell phone.

Christopher does not answer his phone.

"It's me," I say to a thousand volts of mindless

electricity. "I don't know what I'm supposed to be doing here. How does it feel like my heart is being burned right here in my chest, on fire, but I'm not doing anything but sitting here? I need you to... God, Christopher. I just need you. Where are you? Why won't you come?"

CHAPTER TWENTY-TWO

THE GIRL CODE

T HERE'S A COMMOTION in the hallway, and I close my eyes to shut it out. It doesn't go away, though; it gets louder. Voices filter through the fog in my head like rays of too-bright sun.

"The ER is downstairs!"

"She's not here to see a doctor," says a haggard voice in a smooth accent I recognize. "She's here to visit someone. Room three hundred forty-two."

That's where I'm sitting, except why would Hugo have come with Bea? Oh God. I rush into the hallway in time to see my good friend retch into a waste bin. "I'm fine," she mumbles, clearly miserable. And very pregnant. "Ignore me. I'm fine."

"Oh my God." I lean down to stroke her red hair. "I hate you right now. I can't believe you left the hotel for this. You shouldn't have, but I love you."

She laughs weakly. "I thought I could make it."

Beatrix Cartwright has been severely agoraphobic since the death of her parents over a decade ago, not even leaving the penthouse hotel where she practically raised herself ever since. She's been making strides lately—short visits to the Den, to the museum, to a park. Those required a great deal of planning, not a phone call in the middle of the night.

Her usually pale skin has turned a deathly white with a faint greenish tinge. Her eyes are wide in her face when she looks up at me. I suspect her current state has way more to do with being out of her home so unexpectedly, but it can't be good for her. "I'm so sorry," she says.

I think she's apologizing for my mother's condition, but I'm not ready to deal with that, so I pretend it's still about throwing up. "Nonsense. Hugo is the one who should be sorry. I can't believe he let you leave in this condition."

Hugo Bellmont is perpetually cool and effortlessly suave pretty much every time I've met him, but he looks frayed at the edges for maybe the first time ever. His hair is all out of place, his shirt wrinkled. Lines of stress bracket his mouth. "She insisted," he says, and in the hoarseness of his voice I hear every argument he must have made to her.

"I'm glad you're here," I say, and as I say it, I realize it's true. Part of me wants to shove my head into the ground, but that's the cowardly part. The stronger side of me wants my friends to help me through this. "Come inside the room. If you throw up again I'll hold your hair back."

I help her inside, where she looks at my mother's still form on the hospital bed with such a severe expression that I wonder if she's going to throw up again. She must be remembering her own mother. The plane crash. "My God," I whisper. "Was your last memory at the hospital?"

"Close," Hugo says, his expression grim.

"I'm completely fine," Bea says, her voice weak and very much *not* fine. It's only a testament to her loyalty as a friend that she's holding it together, but I feel the fine tremors shake her where I'm helping her stand.

"Sit down at least." The gray cloth chair has questionable stains and is probably permanently molded into the shape of my ass, but at least she stops swaying when she's there.

Hugo kneels down beside her, a look of worry

on his handsome, angular face. There's nothing of the seducer in him now. He looks elemental, all the walls he's built up torn down to reveal a love so raw it hurts to look at it. "Rest, *ma belle*. We're here now, so you can rest for a moment."

"You must be dehydrated." The last inch of coffee in my Styrofoam turned cold and lumpy a while ago. "Sutton went down to the gift shop in search of food a few minutes ago. I'm sure he'll come back with a water bottle or something, or we can send him out again."

Sutton will know how to fix this. That's what he's done for me the past few hours, for the whole time I've known him—found the sharp points in my world and smoothed them down. There's a sense that I'm coasting along in this calm new landscape, closing my eyes as the wind hits my face, blind to the dangers around me.

It's a relief after facing off with a man who turned every edge into a blade.

Bea faced a severe anxiety attack in order to be by my side, and even though I would have told her not to come, I'm touched. In contrast Christopher Bardot cannot even be moved to answer his phone. *Sorry about missing the Death Plan,* he could have sent in a text message, like a sad RSVP to a party he wouldn't be attending.

Instead there's only a ringing silence.

Hugo looks pained. "That's the reason she insisted on coming here."

"I'm so sorry," Bea says, her green eyes filled with regret. "I know it violates the man code but I couldn't break the girl code, and you really needed to know."

"I have no idea what you're talking about."

"The library," Hugo says.

Bea grimaces. "It's never going to be fixed. Sutton lied about that. Maybe he was doing it to protect you. Or maybe he did it for… other reasons. But the construction crew that's there isn't going to be able to salvage it. It's not even safe to be inside."

The words don't make sense. "What?"

"I'm sorry," Hugo says. "He feels bad about it."

"Not bad enough to tell her the truth," Bea says in an arch tone that sounds more like herself than she has in the past few minutes. There's a little pink in her cheeks, too. Indignation looks good on her, but I'm still stuck on the word *lied*.

"Sutton lied to me?"

There's a scuffing sound from behind me, the sole of a shoe against the large square tiles underfoot, and I turn to see Sutton in the doorway, a large paper bag in one hand, a balloon with roses on it trailing behind him in the hallway, bobbing uselessly in the air-conditioner draft.

"Perhaps we should leave them alone," Hugo says, sounding somehow both guilty and accusing. I suppose I should be glad he was willing to defy his friendship in order to tell me the truth, but it feels a little too late—kind of like me reading the Death Plan.

"I'm staying right here," Bea says, but she's completely green now.

"Please go home," I tell her fervently. "I'm only going to worry about you if you stay. And I'm pretty sure Hugo is about to have a stress aneurysm."

She presses her hand to her mouth, eyes squeezes shut. "Honestly. Yes. Okay."

Hugo looks immensely relieved as they give me a hug and kiss to say goodbye. Then I'm left alone in the room with the man I can't quite look in the eye. I'm not sure whether I'm mad at him. Yes, I decide. I would be mad if I had any energy in my body to feel things.

"Why didn't you tell me the truth?" I ask, but the question feels far away.

"Would you have let me stay if I had?"

I shake my head, but it's not really an answer. It's too hard to think in this room with people, even if it's just one person. One person I shared my body with. Maybe even my heart, but never fully my trust. Maybe I knew Christopher was telling the truth about the library.

There's only one man I've ever really trusted, even though I shouldn't. I'm not sure if that makes me foolish or in love. Is there even a difference? I love Christopher, but like my mother's love for my father, it doesn't mean anything good. Love is a chain around my ankle. It's an anchor bearing me to the bottom of the ocean.

It's this feeling of brokenness as I watch my mother die.

CHAPTER TWENTY-THREE

PROTESTING

S HE WAKES UP so calm and casual it's like
nothing is wrong. "Harper."

There's a lurch in my throat, and I can taste
stale coffee and hope. "Mom! You're awake. Let
me call the nurse. Are you in pain? Are you
hungry?"

"No—Harper, wait. I don't need anything."

My stomach sinks. "What can I do?"

"Can you just…?" She blinks, a little too fast
to be normal. "I lied about the plan. About being
okay with everything. I'm afraid, baby, but it
doesn't hurt anymore."

Tears leak down my face. There's no pantry or
closet to hide in. No pillow to scream my pain
into. There's only her thin body to hold, and she
holds me back, her hands shaking.

"I was—" She pauses, seeming to struggle to find the words. "I was looking up. With your father I was looking up, and I could never walk again."

For a terrible moment I think she might be hallucinating, not really with me even though she seems clearer now than she has in months. Except I don't think she's hallucinating. She was looking up, like Deborah Kerr in the movie. She was hit by a car because she was so in love. What a cautionary tale, that movie. It had a happy ending, though.

Not like my mother's love life. "I'm so sorry," I whisper.

"Don't be—sorry." She grasps my hand, her head falling back, eyes closed. The distance widens between us, and I hold her tighter. "Love you. That's the plan."

And then she goes quiet.

The *beep beep beep* keeps going. No one rushes into the room, but there might as well be a ghost in the room with me. That's how quiet and still my mother's body is. That's how lifeless she looks. There are a thousand cracks in my foundation, but this one is the deepest. I press my face into her body, into the warmth that isn't quite alive, and cry.

The little squiggles on the machine bump up regularly enough, but that's just electricity. Those are electrons firing inside a circuit. That's not what makes my mother a person. That part is already gone, so it's not a surprise when she starts breathing in a terrible sound that fills the room. A good thing, Freida says when she hears it. It means my mother is so relaxed that she can no longer be bothered to wake up. She is too relaxed to live. Can you imagine that?

That death is just the ultimate spa vacation, after all.

The afternoon sun presses hot against my neck, squeezing through the cheap white blinds on the window, marking my skin in a completely random place. The middle of the day seems like a strange time to die, but that's when the horrible sound of her breathing stops.

When she's so relaxed she leaves me completely alone, as if it had been so much effort to stay with me as long as she did. Every piece of art I've ever made flashes in front of me—empty, empty. There's nothing to explain the hollowness of this room.

The hollowness of my heart.

All that protesting did not accomplish anything—I couldn't save the library. I couldn't save my mother. I hold her hand where it rests on the bed, and it's still warm. A lie, because she's gone. Her body is still. Her chest does not rise and fall.

Eventually the nurse comes and makes the machine stop beeping. She puts her hands on my shoulder, but she doesn't insist that I leave. That must be part of the Death Plan, which suddenly strikes me as funny.

I start laughing, and then Christopher is there. "Harper," he says.

"You're a dream. You aren't real."

"I'm sorry," he says, and it sounds like he means it. Like he's really sorry that I'm alone, even though he's the one who made me this way.

"Why didn't you come?" I say, my words garbled by the grief in my throat, the tears in my eyes. The black in my heart. "You should have come. She asked you to. She wanted you to."

"She didn't," he says with a sigh that is a thousand years old.

I hit his chest with my fists, but he may as well be made of granite. Granite like his eyes. Black and hard and cold. "I hate you. I hate you. I hate you."

He lets me hit him until I collapse. His arms are around me, and I shatter.

CHAPTER TWENTY-FOUR

INEVITABLE

THE HOUSE IS dark when Christopher's car pulls into the drive. How many times have I come here after working late in the library? I shouldn't have been in the library, though. It wasn't safe, which feels ridiculous right now. Who cares about safety? Death is inevitable.

I'm Scarlett come home after the war, the place a husk of its former self. The walls aren't blackened with fire, but they might as well be. The house rings hollow.

Christopher puts me to bed with gentle insistence, undressing me like I'm a child. I press my face into his chest and breathe deep, taking comfort I don't deserve from his scent. My mouth opens to taste him, to bite him. I would swallow him whole if I could, but he sets me back an inch. "Not tonight," he says, and I hiss at him like an animal.

"Yes, tonight." This is when I need him—rough and animalistic. If he won't hurt me then I'll hurt him. It's the only thing that makes sense in this topsy turvy night. It's the only thing I can trust.

I grasp his shirt and press myself against him, my lips mashing his. It's isn't graceful or seductive. There's a violence inside me that needs to get out. I bite at his lips, but it seems to work. It seems to work because his breath catches. His body goes stock still—not in the way where he's fighting me.

He's still in the way where he's fighting himself.

I give him a rough shove, and he lets himself step back. "Fight me," I say, panting.

A low growl. "You don't want this."

I want it to stop hurting inside me, and maybe if he hits me, maybe if he hurts me, I won't be able to feel the ache on the inside anymore. All I need is one minute of relief. All I need is one minute to forget. I step forward and raise my hand—he catches my wrist.

His face is in an inch from mine. "You don't want this," he says again, but this time it doesn't sound like concern for me. It sounds like a threat, and my body responds with a rush of adrenaline. My heart pounds ten thousand seconds in the time it takes him to let me go.

And then I'm on him, climbing his body, knocking him to the floor. He cushions my fall with his body, his grunt half pain, half pleasure. I scratch my nails down his chest, and even through the fabric of his shirt I know I've drawn blood. A sound escapes me—something angry and grieving and wild.

He should be scared of me right now. I'm a little scared of this. God knows Sutton would be; he only ever treated me like a lady. Skittish like his beautiful golden horse, but a lady nonetheless.

Nothing about this is ladylike. It's not even human, this grief inside me.

Christopher doesn't look shocked. He looks at me like I'm the same as always, like he always knew that I'm a she-devil, a siren. A mythical creature with eyes that will turn a mortal man to stone.

He isn't mortal. He burns under my gaze. "Go ahead," he says from the floor, leaning back, offering up his body to me. "Take what you need. Let me give it to you."

The words should be enough to jolt me back to sanity, but I'm too far gone. I gasp him everywhere, everywhere, my nails raking him, my teeth bared to him. He pushes his hands above his head on the floor, as if they're chained there. As if he's Prometheus and I'm the fury of the gods, torturing him until the end of time. And he likes it. He likes it.

I rock my hips over the hardness pressing his jeans. He jerks against me, unable to hold still at the heat of my covered sex, at the rock of my body, even though he accepted my pain in silence.

My head falls back, and I close my eyes. It's like water to let my hips move over him, liquid movement, the path of least resistance to rub my clit against his erection. Pleasure arcs through my body, sharp through the muted agony. It's almost unbearable, the friction too much. I make myself feel it, and my climax rises with an overwhelming hurt that comes from deep inside. I rock and rock and rock—and against him with a terrible cry and tears streaming down my cheeks.

It fills my head, the knowledge that I will never see her again. We'll never watch an old movie. She'll never tell me that I'm strong and brave and good, because I'm not, I can't be. I collapse on Christoper's battered chest, sobbing salt-tears into his cuts.

His arms come around me, and he soothes me

with nonsense words, with soft caresses. I know with certainty then that no frat boy, no other man could have withstood me. Only this man, more god than human. He absorbs all my grief and pain into his body, and I know he's strong enough for more.

I cry against him for what I've lost, but more than that I cry for what was never found.

For the love my mother never had. For the peace and security in those black-and-white movies that never came true—and now they never can come true. She'll never know how it feels to be held forever.

And the worst part is, Daddy never knew it either.

They could have been everything together. Instead they were nothing.

The fabric beneath my cheek is drenched in tears. The floor hard beneath my knees. Through my tears I come to realize that we're lying on the floor, my body draped over Christopher's, his cock still hard between my legs. "I'm sorry," I mumble, reaching for him, fumbling. "Sorry."

I'm not sure what I can offer him with my heart still broken, not sure why he's even still aroused when my eyes are red and puffy like this, but he stops me with a sharp sound.

"Absolutely not." His voice is rough with need, but his tone leaves no room for argument. As if we can't cross some invisible line of sexual ethics that says I'm allowed to rub myself off on his body, but he himself can't come. It's ridiculous, especially when he's throbbing the inside of my thigh. He must be in pain. But then he pulls me down to his body again, pushes my head on his shoulder. I sink into the cradle of his body. That's all I needed—an orgasm, fast and rough. A forceful cuddle. And sleep claims me, dragging me down into the inky black.

CHAPTER TWENTY-FIVE

TROPHY

WHEN I WAKE up again, it's the middle of the night.

Christopher's face looks softer in the moonlight. This man has been jerked around by my family, his life twisting at our whims. First my father's will and then my mother's Death Plan. He's so beautiful and tortured. Maybe the best thing I can do is finally leave him alone.

Last night feels like a dream.

The only thing I know for sure is that I can't stay in this house.

I'm half asleep as I find my keys and head out the door—without my purse or my phone. I don't need those things, not for what I need to do. Not for where I need to go. Isn't that what a library used to be? A place where you didn't need money to read. Where you didn't need the newest, biggest iPhone to learn something about the world.

An outdated idea. A defunct building. The world still needs books and knowledge, but it's not going to get them here at the long-closed Tanglewood Library.

There's no saving it.

No saving me.

The library looks almost sinister in the moonlight with its rough planes and jagged edges. The girl stands at the corner, selling her body. She's breaking apart, just like the building. I should give her whatever cash is in my wallet—except I didn't bring my purse. There's nothing but my hands now. That's all I ever had, the ability to create. The ability to destroy.

Harper St. Claire distilled down into a single goal.

She gives me a strange look, a little concerned, mostly wary. Like an alley cat I've disturbed in the middle of her dinner. "What are you doing here?" she spits.

"What is anyone doing here?"

"I'm trying to stay alive."

"Same, girl. Same." I don't have a death wish; I never did. I want to stay alive, to *feel* alive, and there are only two things that have ever done that—Christopher and art. I'm in a destructive mood, and I've already torn up his chest, so now it will have to be art.

Not anything as clean and pure as *creating* art.

Tonight is about falling off a yacht.

"You don't know anything about what I have to do to survive." Something in her reminds me of me with Christopher—defensive, because she's been hurt before. Because people who've been hurt like knowing it will happen again. There's comfort in the familiar.

"You're right," I say, because the library isn't going to help. What is it a monument to except for the way things used to be? For the patriarchy and the goddamn men who keep this girl on her knees instead of building and creating and living without fear.

She disappears around the corner, leaving me on the sidewalk.

It's easy enough to slip through the temporary barriers. The wall seems more majestic at night. A beautiful lie, because it will never survive what comes next. I'm furious that it let me believe, even for a moment. Part of me knows I'm not thinking straight, but the other part is sure that's a good thing. I've had too much straight thinking. Tonight I'm all the way twisted.

The ladders are propped against the sides of the library. The scaffolding stands where I can reach it, but I need something more than height and clay tonight.

Out back there are vehicles the construction crew leaves behind. Most of the tools are stored in a white van, which is locked. This isn't a safe neighborhood after all. Luckily I learned some very bad things over the years, including how to pick a lock. With a bent wire hanger in the doors at the back, I manage to get it open.

I have my pick of weapons—a shovel. A crowbar. Yes, that will work.

It's almost too easy to climb onto the scaffolding that's waiting for me at the back of the library. I plunge the sharp end of the crowbar into the crack and lever my whole body, throwing my weight against the iron. Wood splits with a satisfying *thwak*.

I keep breaking the wall until my hair is full of wood shards.

Thwak.

Keep fighting the wood until it comes apart.

Thwak.

I lose track of time doing this, lose track of my limbs and muscles. Lose track of my thoughts. Even so it's not quite a surprise when I feel the metal beneath my feet shiver. Christopher climbs onto the scaffold with me, but I ignore him. There are splinters in my hands. I only feel them when he pries the bar from me.

"Look what you've done," he murmurs, smoothing a thumb over my bloodied palm.

I swallow the pain. "Better me than you."

He swears softly. "Is this what I've done to you?"

"No,' I say, but that feels like a lie. It's made me feel crazy to love a man who won't love me back. To have him look at me like he's burning alive for me, only for him to push me away.

"Come with me."

"But—" I want to keep going until the building comes down on me. Isn't that what everyone said would happen? Without a yellow hard hat on my head. I would buried.

I want to be buried right now.

Christopher doesn't take me back to the *Gone with the Wind* house.

Instead we pull up at a contemporary home making angles over a sloping hill. I step inside and stare dully at the large piece of rubble with Cleopatra's eye. It doesn't seem strange that he should have it. Of course he paid some exorbitant amount of money online. Lord knows he made much more money from the deal than that.

It's a trophy.

"Why do you have that?"

"It took some convincing to get the buyer to part with it."

"I don't understand."

"You take that crow bar to me, if that's what you need to do. It's my skin you wanted to break open, and God, you have every right to do that. I never should have closed myself to you."

I can't hold onto the anger. It slips through my fingers, leaving only the grief. I would rather be fighting the wall, becoming bloody and hurt. I'd rather anything than this terrible emptiness. "This is another game. Another conquest. Another way to make me love you and then push me away. I won't survive it, Christopher."

"You'll survive anything," he says, a little sadly. "Even the terrible way I love you."

My breath catches. I want to argue with him, but part of me always knew it. "I hate you. I hate you." The words blur together, and then I'm crying. The words change. "I love you."

He leads me farther into the house, and I stop in front of a fireplace almost large enough to stand in. And above it there's the Medusa I painted from the art show all those years ago.

"I should have made you mine then, Harper. You *were* mine, even then."

He lowers his lips to mine, and I tilt my head up to meet him. I'm done fighting this, done destroying things, done making trophies for him to collect. And I know that he won't push me away again, not because he'll never retreat. Because I won't let him. I'm not only a woman. I'm a she-devil. A siren. A mythical creature, except I'm the one who's been made of stone. And he's the man who turns me into flesh and blood.

CHAPTER TWENTY-SIX
DESTRUCTION

THE WRECKING BALL slams into the building, the sound deafening.

Dust rises around us, stinging my eyes. I'm not happy about the destruction. It feels a little like death, but sometimes you need to die so you can start over again. There's a crowd behind us—our friends, Bea and Hugo. Avery and Gabriel.

There's a community behind us.

Christopher squeezes my hand. "Are you okay?" he asks, though it's less of a sound with the rumble still falling in front of us and a hard hat obscuring my hearing. It's the only way he let me within two miles of the construction site today. It's more the way his lips move.

The whole thing is coming down, along with every hope I ever had for it, every wall I ever built around myself. Leaving room for something new.

I nod to him, squeezing his hand back. "Because you're with me." He shouldn't be able to hear me either, but there's no mistaking the satisfaction in his onyx eyes. It's the same as when I wake up beside him in bed. The same as when I spread my legs above his mouth. Because he didn't only need to save me.

He needed me to save him, too.

I reach up on my tiptoes, and he obliged by bending down. Gentle, gentle, even though there's a wildness inside me, I tug at the lobe of his ear with my teeth. "Diabolical," I murmur, though he probably only feels a whisper of breath. "You wanted this all along."

And when he straightens, his eyes brim with the lazy pleasure of a man who's recently come, his body sated, his mind at ease. "Yes," he says, the word unmistakable.

My heart snags on something close to the surface.

Love, I think.

Through the cloud of destruction, you can make out vivid colors peeking through. Dust settles in slow degrees, the way a sun would set, crouching low to the ground and then gone. In its wake we have a full view of Christopher's luxury condo building, with its walls of glass along the ground floor and concrete above. A woman stands proud and unashamed of her breasts, her wings, her wild mane of hair. Lilith is a demon and a sex goddess—the heart of female defiance.

She was the first woman created, even before Eve, made from the same dirt as Adam. Was she cast out of the garden for disobedience? Or did she leave in search of greener pastures?

Is she a deviant pleasure-hungry whore?

Or is she simply a woman who wants freedom?

They are the same story, depending on who tells the tale.

And in my story, she finds her own garden, in the glorious foliage and flowers surrounding her. Because Freida was telling the truth. Death is a natural part of life. And like the burning of a field, this library will give rise to new birth.

There's more light now, with the building gone, and we'll need those rays of sun for the garden we're going to plan here. I can already see trees and bushes and flowers—but the painting against the wall will remain as the cornerstone. The beginning. It's my most ambitious work to date. And it wasn't completely a secret. It took me three weeks to paint the plants that curl up from the glass wall and hang down from giant illusory trees. It took that long with elaborate, very safe scaffolding and rope around my waist and a crew to prime the wall and seal it after.

It's only Lilith who came at the end, working at night, with only Christopher beside me. My arms feel like jelly after working for twelve hours straight. There's still paint smudged across my arms and shoved under my fingernails. Christopher doesn't look much better—there's specks of blue in his black hair from where I gripped it in a celebratory kiss, which turned into more, twenty feet above the ground on top of our large stable scaffold. There are faint lines under his eyes from being awake all night, but he looks live-wire and alert. Maybe watching for a threat since not everyone in the city is happy about the image of female empowerment painted on the building. Not everyone wants the west side to be restored. There are true demons that lurk these streets, but Lilith will help find them.

I saved her eyes for last, because they had to watch over the park. And they had to look out over the west side of Tanglewood. It's her domain, all of it. There will be a modern library worthy of Smith College. There will be a soup kitchen and a shelter so that young women have choices. That will be the practical side, the necessary side—and finally, the perfect use for my trust fund. I've always been a fan of grand gestures. Of symbolism.

Of proving to the world that women don't need to be meek to be beautiful—and that's why Lilith will remain standing throughout all of it.

I was wrong to think that we needed a structure to house her. She isn't afraid of the elements. Sometimes you need the darkness to shine. And sometimes you need death to come fully alive. Sunlight beams across the paint, drying her eyes. She looks on with a knowledge hard-won and peace that comes from finally finding home.

Thank You for Reading

Thank you so much for reading THE EVOLUTION OF MAN!

I hope you loved the duet! This was a personal and painful story to write because of what happens with Harper's mother, but I'm so glad that I can share it with you. Harper's book was the most requested after she first appeared in THE PAWN, and now her story is complete.

If you're wondering what happened to Sutton, I'm going to send out a FREE bonus epilogue about him. Sign up here: www.skyewarren.com/bonus

You can read Hugo and Bea's story right now! Find out what happens when a seductive and jaded male escort shows up at the penthouse of an innocent heiress...

> "Escort is stunningly sexy and staggeringly heartfelt–gorgeously written and saturated with pure, unadulterated desire. Five Mon Dieu stars!"
>
> – Sierra Simone, USA Today bestselling author

And the USA Today bestselling virgin auction book THE PAWN with Gabriel and Avery in Tanglewood is on all retailers! *There's one way to save our house, one thing I have left of value—my body...*

Keep reading for a sneak peek of Escort...

THE CITY LOOKS beautiful at night, its rough edges kissed by moonlight, bright neon lights full of hope. My Bugatti slices through the darkness, smooths over cracked downtown streets. The leather is warm on the steering wheel, the gears smooth under my control. Every muscle in my body hums with anticipation, the certainty that I'm going to get laid tonight. It's more than sex that gets me off. It's the journey. Discovering what makes a woman work. What holds her back and what lets her go.

I pull into the valet driveway and toss my keys to Alejandro, who has three kids at home and another one on the way. "Take care of her," I tell him, slipping a twenty into his palm.

"It's my pleasure," he says, giving the gleaming curves an admiring look.

She's gorgeous, this car. The first thing I purchased for myself once I was done scrabbling for scraps. Once I learned how to use my particular talents. Her form is both sleek and curvy, the kind of body that drives a man to his knees. But it's not the way she looks that I love best. It's the way she moves. The engine that has a mind of her own, sometimes sweet surrender, sometimes temperamental.

I love her best when she gives me a challenge.

L'Etoile is a luxury hotel with 24-karat gold chandeliers and white marble floors. A slice of European aesthetic in the center of Tanglewood's urban sprawl. It's garish and expensive, which suits me fine. It was founded in the '40s by a woman who claimed to be French nobility. In reality, she was the madame of a lucrative brothel.

That suits me fine, as well.

The front counter is carved with ornate scrolls and baby angels. A woman stands behind them. Jessica, her name tag says. I give her a winning smile, and her brown eyes widen. "Good evening to you. Is there perhaps a message left for me? Hugo Bellmont."

Her expression becomes soft, vulnerable. I should be very tired of this expression, especially when it comes so easily, but my male pride is a simple creature. It does not mind making women swoon, again and again.

"I… I can check for you." She looks around for a moment, almost dazed. As if it's never occurred to her that people might come to the desk for messages.

"You have my gratitude."

After some fumbling, her cheeks deeply pink, she locates a stack of envelopes in one of the little cubbies. There is one with black script that I can recognize as my name from here. "Here you are."

I think about what would be required to undress her, to take off her clothes and what remains of her defenses. Very little, but we would both enjoy the journey. Alas, she isn't my intended partner tonight.

Inside the envelope is a hotel key card, which leads to the penthouse.

I've been to a hundred penthouses inside the city. And several outside of it. Each one is its own brand of ridiculous luxury. That's part of the heavy price tag, the ridiculousness. Bathtubs that could fit a baby elephant. Private infinity pools. A helipad complete with exclusive helicopter usage. You don't spring for the penthouse unless you want to be wowed.

Somehow, I've never been to the penthouse in

L'Etoile.

It's always eluded me. And haunted me.

It isn't the amenities that interest me. A bed made of solid gold. Draperies spun from a rare Chinese silkworm. Whatever they are I'm sure they're lovely, but it's the person who rents them I want to meet. My chest feels tight with anticipation. A heavy beat through my veins, because this is more than a client. This is someone who might have access to the current owner of this hotel.

I shouldn't get my hopes up, but hopes aren't under my control. They rise and rise, high enough that I have to turn my thoughts away from revenge. To something much more base. Sex.

There's a private elevator that leads only to the penthouse and the private rooftop gardens. It requires the key card to call it down. There are three buttons on the inside wood panel: L for lobby, P for penthouse, and R for the roof. There's also the silhouette of a bell. I suppose that's for if, in the space between the lobby and their suite, they decide they need champagne and strawberries delivered. I could call down for some. Or I could have brought some flowers. Props, you could say. Props to charm a lady, but I don't need them. Don't want them. I pride myself on making them feel like they're the most incredible woman

I've ever met, because for one night, they are.

A soft chime signals my arrival. The doors slide open.

I was prepared for any type of penthouse decor. Something lush and antique to match the lower floors. Something modern and sleek to appeal to the upscale traveler.

What I'm looking at isn't a penthouse at all. Not one I've ever seen.

There's a lumpy corduroy sofa in front of a gilded brick fireplace. A pile of old books about to topple over on a side table that probably came from Ikea. Through the room I can see floor-to-ceiling windows that would have been the focal point, but they've been covered by drapes. That alone would not be remarkable, except for the string of star-shaped plastic lights that traipse across them. It takes me a moment to realize that my mouth is open. Shocked. I'm shocked, which is pleasant enough considering it's a novelty. How long has it been since something surprised me? And where is the object of that surprise? There is no woman to greet me. No seductress. No glamourous woman ready for the night of her life. God, what is that strange tightening in my chest? It feels like anticipation, deep and true, and it's been a lifetime since I felt that.

"Hello," I call, stepping into the suite.

There's a thump from the bedroom. A woman pops her head around the corner, all frizzy hair and wild eyes and plump pink lips. She wears a black dress with a startling high neck, lace on top, the kind that a matron would wear—but her skin is perfectly smooth, her eyes wide. This is a young woman. Younger than myself, her clothes an anachronism. Her expression? Pure relief. "Oh thank God."

She sounds so sincere that I have visions of an orgasm emergency. A deficiency so intense she had to dial a twenty-four-hour line to have it fixed. There's something undeniably hot about the idea of a woman in dire straits and me the only one who can help.

"Hugo Bellmont," I tell her, providing a small bow. "At your service."

And then I give her the smile. Not the megawatt one that I used downstairs. I give her the slow, suggestive one that lets her know every dirty thing that I'm thinking.

It isn't fake. It doesn't need to be. Not with her whispery curls that I'd love to feel in my fist. Not with the pale freckles across her nose that I'd love to track all the way down her body.

Her eyes are an interesting pale green. I want

to look in them while I go down on her.

Every single dirty thought is in the smallest smile.

Except she disappears back into the bedroom. "In here!"

How unusual. I've never met a woman as hurried about her sexual requirements. She sounds worried, almost frantic, and I haven't even been here sixty seconds.

I follow her, feeling for the first time in years out of my depth. It's a nice feeling, a pleasant simmer in my veins. My steps feel lighter across the plush carpet.

At the threshold I barely have time to register the strange furniture. It's large and antique. Expensive but mismatched. As if they crammed an estate sale into one room.

The young woman is bent over a large dresser, her ass perfectly plump. I could fill my hands with her. Could press my new erection against the crease. Except it isn't a sexy pose.

Instead she seems to be looking *behind* the dresser.

"It's okay," she's saying, breathless. "Come out, sweetie. You can do it."

Based on the sweet tone of her voice and the cat dish I spotted on the way inside, I already know what I'm going to see when I peek over the top of the dresser. Sure enough, there's a fluffy cat with bright yellow eyes peering up at me.

I don't have much experience with cats. They were one level up from rodents where I grew up, useful for catching rats and underfoot in dark alleys.

However, my experience with pussies of a different sort translates just fine, because I can see exactly what's happened to the poor girl. She's backed herself all the way into a corner, made her body so small she can't possibly come out.

No matter how nicely her owner coaxes her, it won't work. It can't possibly. Something like this isn't solved with words; it's solved with a confident, calming touch.

I straighten enough to pull off my jacket. "If you'll allow me."

The woman glances back at me, her eyes going wide as she sees my forearms where I'm rolling up my sleeves. "What are you going to do?"

"I assume you wish me to retrieve the cat."

"Rescue her," she corrects. "Because you have long arms."

I've had women compliment my length before, but usually they're referring to a different body part. Nothing about this night is usual;

maybe that's why I like it so much. "Happy to be of service."

"She's very nervous. She might scratch you."

"Wouldn't be the first time." I give her a small smile, and this time I'm rewarded by a pinkening of her cheeks. "Now if you would move aside. I require room to work."

She scoots herself around me, careful not to touch, sucking in her breath as she passes by me. Is she afraid of me? I don't think so. At least not the ordinary fear a woman might have of a man. Instead she seems wary, much like the cat that watches me from behind the dresser, nervous of the world and its unknowns, terrified of everything and nothing at all.

With both hands braced on the side of the dresser, I use all my strength to lift it. As I suspected it's an ancient piece, made back when they used solid wood for every beam and joint. It probably weighs a thousand pounds, which is why the woman didn't move it first. I manage to move it two inches farther from the wall, which isn't enough for a person to walk behind, but is enough for a cat. This one would probably wander out eventually, when she wants to eat, but I don't think my client will relax until she does.

So I return to the far end of the dresser, near

the corner, and bend to look at the cat. She stares at me, her eyes almost glowing, unfathomable. "You're a beauty, aren't you?" I murmur.

No response. She doesn't even blink.

"I could talk to you for hours," I say, reaching down to stroke the top of her head.

She's soft and unexpectedly fragile beneath all that fur. It's almost like armor, the thickness of it. It makes her seem larger than she is. "I could talk for hours, and you still wouldn't trust me, would you? You won't believe a thing I say, so I'll just have to show you."

I don't change the cadence of my voice, not even as I reach below the cat and scoop her up, not even as I clasp her securely against my chest and pet her head. She curls against me with a faint purr of relief, her thick tail swishing back and forth in gratitude.

"Oh my God, thank you," the woman says, looking torn between snatching her cat away and coming near me. Quite a dilemma, she has. "I realized I couldn't find her thirty minutes ago, and then spent all this time looking, and then when I did find her she wouldn't come out." She stops herself, flushing. "Sorry, I babble when I'm nervous."

And it's adorable, but I know better than to

tell her that.

"My assistance does come with a price," I say instead.

Her eyes widen. "Oh?"

"Your name. It's only fair now that I'm holding your pussy."

Oh, the color of her cheeks. They remind me of sunsets with wind from the west, the kind that herald good weather for sailors the following day. "Bee," she says.

"The kind that make honey?"

"No, Bea like Beatrix." She makes a face. "It was my grandmother's name."

I would love to say a name as unique as Beatrix while I pound into her, but it's clear she'd rather I called her by the nickname. Anyway, it suits her. Simple on the surface, a thousand meanings beneath. "It's a pleasure to meet you, Bea. And your cat," I prompt.

"Minette," she answers, her expression softening.

Upon hearing her name, the cat seems to realize she's been far too content in a stranger's arms. She pulls herself away, a little haughty, and leaps onto the floor. Only then, from the relative safety of two feet away, does she turn back to give me a warning hiss.

Then she swishes away with a walk I can only admire.

"I suppose I haven't made a friend," I say ruefully.

Bea grins. "Are you kidding? She didn't take a swipe at you. I'm pretty sure that means she loves you in Minette language. She doesn't like new people."

Why do you travel with a cat who dislikes new people? I suppose she could keep her locked up in penthouse suites around the country, wealthy enough to insist that her cat sit with her in first class instead of locked in steerage, but it still seems like a strange pet to travel with.

Come to think of it, the pet isn't the only thing strange. The old furniture. The young woman who's looking at me with a mixture of trepidation and hope.

"Is it possible..." I say, almost reluctant to ask, but needing to know. "That she doesn't meet a lot of people because she *lives* on the top floor of an exclusive boutique hotel?"

Green eyes blink at me, as wide as the ones that looked at me from behind the dresser. As if I've trapped her there. As if I'm the only one who can get her out. "Ah. Yes." She laughs a little. "What gave it away?"

A million things, but mostly the fact that Bea

looks so skittish I think I could spook her if I move too fast. I nod toward a painting on the wall, which features a smaller version of Minette in pointillism. "I assume it's not standard concierge service to paint a masterpiece of the guest's pet. Though if it is you really have to mention that in the Expedia review."

She laughs, the sound light as air, making my chest feel full. "I'm guessing Olivier would rather paint her than clean her litterbox."

So she's on a first-name basis with the concierge. It means she's been living here for a while, most likely, which is interesting because she can't be older than twenty. The high-necked dress is strange for someone that young, but it's surprisingly sexy. It conforms to her figure, emphasizing her curves and making my blood run hot.

Her smile fades. "It's not a problem, is it? Me living here?"

As quickly as that, my profession fills the air like smoke. Like a bomb went off.

"It's no problem," I assure her. The agency will send me to a hotel room as easily as a client's high-rise condo. There's no difference as long as the credit card charge goes through.

A male escort. His virgin client. What happens when one night isn't enough?

I'm an escort, which means this date is nothing more than a mutually enjoyable transaction. There shouldn't be any surprises, not for one as jaded as me, but when I walk into the penthouse suite of L'Etoile, everything changes.

1) For one thing, Bea is heartstoppingly gorgeous. Pale green eyes and endless freckles. Curves I want to spend all night exploring, as if her body was made for me.

2) Her innocence makes me want to use my entire inventory of bedroom tricks on her and then invent a few more.

3) Except that... she's a virgin.

I can initiate her into the world of desire without letting her get attached, can't I? A few hours of tutoring, and at the end of the night a small fortune will be deposited into my bank account.

But once I realize one night with her won't be enough, I'm the one who's screwed.

Want to read more? You can find ESCORT on Amazon.com, Barnes & Noble NOOK, iBooks, Kobo, and Google Play!

Books by Skye Warren

Endgame trilogy & Masterpiece Duet
The Pawn
The Knight
The Castle
The King
The Queen

Underground series
Rough Hard Fierce
Wild Dirty Secret
Sweet
Deep

Stripped series
Tough Love
Love the Way You Lie
Better When It Hurts
Even Better
Pretty When You Cry
Caught for Christmas
Hold You Against Me
To the Ends of the Earth

Criminals and Captives standalones

Prisoner

Hostage

Standalone Dangerous Romance

Wanderlust

On the Way Home

Beauty and the Beast

Anti Hero

Escort

For a complete listing of Skye Warren books, visit

www.skyewarren.com/books

About the Author

Skye Warren is the New York Times bestselling author of dangerous romance such as the Endgame trilogy. Her books have been featured in Jezebel, Buzzfeed, USA Today Happily Ever After, Glamour, and Elle Magazine. She makes her home in Texas with her loving family, sweet dogs, and evil cat.

Sign up for Skye's newsletter:
www.skyewarren.com/newsletter

Like Skye Warren on Facebook:
facebook.com/skyewarren

Join Skye Warren's Dark Room reader group:
skyewarren.com/darkroom

Follow Skye Warren on Instagram:
instagram.com/skyewarrenbooks

Visit Skye's website for her current booklist:
www.skyewarren.com

Copyright

The Evolution of Man © 2018 by Skye Warren
Print Edition

Cover design by Book Beautiful
Formatted by BB eBooks